FIELDWORK IN UKRAINIAN SEX

Forthcoming titles by Oksana Zabuzhko:
Museum of Abandoned Secrets
Oh Sister, My Sister

FIELDWORK IN UKRAINIAN SEX

OKSANA ZABUZHKO

TRANSLATED BY Halyna Hryn

PUBLISHED BY

amazoncrossing

Fieldwork in Ukrainian Sex by Oksana Zabuzhko was first published in
1996 by Zhoda in Kyiv as *Pol´ovi doslidzhennia z ukraïns´koho seksu*.
An excerpt from *Fieldwork in Ukrainian Sex* appeared in *AGNI* 53,
Spring 2001.

Translated from the Ukrainian by Halyna Hryn.
First published in English in 2011 by AmazonCrossing.

Published by AmazonCrossing
P.O. Box 400818
Las Vegas, NV 89140

ISBN-13: 9781611090086
ISBN-10: 1611090083
Library of Congress Control Number: 2010918615

Not today, she says to herself. Not yet, not today. In the kitchen—a tiny, "eat-in" kitchen (refrigerator, hotplate, cupboard with carelessly tacked-on doors determined to open every time you turn your back like a loose jaw on a paralyzed face, and all this separated off by a medium-height stand made of wooden planks that looks like something you might normally find in a bar—this "counter" allows you to serve meals directly from the narrow enclosure into the room—sure, why not!—like morning coffee, for example, or a little roast chicken for lunch, just like the ones in the television commercials: golden crisp on the outside, juicy on the inside, legs playfully tucked in and presented on a bed of lettuce—these chickens always look much happier than live ones, simply radiating a deep blush of pleasure at the prospect of being eaten—you can also serve juice, or perhaps gin and tonic in a tall thick glass, you can add ice, the cubes sound so funny when they rattle as you pour them into the glass, or you can do it without ice, and in fact the possibilities are endless, but you just need one thing—for there to be *someone sitting* on the other side of their fucking counter, in which, incidentally, a colony of ants seems to have made a home, because every once in a while you've got something crawling around on the Formica that really doesn't belong in a hygienic American home, nor in a non-American one, come to think of it—someone to whom you could serve all this good stuff as you smile your cover-girl smile.

Since, however, there is no one sitting there, nor is there about to be, you've gone ahead and decided to create an improvised winter garden on that counter comprising two innocent potted plants—three weeks ago, when you first moved in here, they were: a luscious, deep-green clump topped with orange flowers—that's one of them—and a thick necklace of shiny, kind of plasticky red nubs on tall stems with elegantly tapered leaves—that's the other. Now both plants have the appearance of having been watered with sulfuric acid for the last three weeks—in place of the rich clump only a few yellow leaves with unevenly singed edges hang like dog ears, and the former tight red beads more and more with every day resemble dried rosehips that someone has decided to stick on burned-out spikes for some unknown reason—the funniest thing is that you deliberately did not forget to water your "winter garden," you nurtured it just like Voltaire had taught, you bet, you *wanted* for there to be another living entity in this apartment, the last of hell only knows how many, your temporary home, where the filth of all previous inhabitants has indelibly settled into every crack so that you didn't even try to wash it out—however, the damned American weeds turned out to be too delicate to withstand your depression, which thickens, unstirred, inside these four walls day by day, so they went ahead and died on you, and you can water them or not water them as you wish—and you still have hopes of keeping people in here!)—so, as I was saying, in this kitchen you've got water dripping from the tap into the sink with a taunting dumb burble and there is no bloody way to drown out that sound—you can't even play a tape because your portable cassette player has gone on the blink. True, somewhere outside the window, which is as narrow as those cupboard doors that keep opening, and quite dark at this hour (you don't bother lowering the blinds, because across from you there's a dead wall anyway), on the other side of the screen an invisible grasshopper chirks like a distant telephone, as though it's stuck right in the screen itself—just the same way that that thought keeps chirking inside your head, or maybe that's in fact the only thing that's chirking—why not do it today, after all, why wait, *what for?*

If you think about it logically, there's nothing at all to wait for. Nothing whatsoever.

Half a bottle of sedatives plus one razor blade, and—please forgive the unsuccessful debut. I tried my very best, with best of intentions, and since the result was a total disaster the honorable thing is to do is fold your cards—I'm not much of a player even now, and it's only going to get worse from here on in: no relief in sight, and my strength's not what it used to be: not a kid anymore.

And yet—no, not today.

Wait a bit longer. See how this film ends. Unlike those that they broadcast here on "public channels," where in the tensest moments as you watch, with involuntary chills of fear, as the hero races down an empty tunnel where from around the bend the most frightening of monsters is about to pounce on him, it suddenly hits you—shit!—everything's going to turn out just fine—another two-three minutes, a confrontation, a pile of swinging limbs, some rolling around on the floor, and the beast, with an outlandish cry, by some miracle transforms to dust, while the masculine and only slightly ruffled hero, enveloped in smoke from the conflagration and breathing heavily, draws the rescued Sharon Stone to his chest, or that other beauty, what's her name, the brunette—and your overwhelming surge of fear is suddenly revealed in all its ridiculousness: once again those Hollywood guys have succeeded, if only for a moment, in suckering you—unlike those, the film that you still can't bring yourself to shut off does not necessarily have to have a happy ending. Still, turning it off is unforgivable bad taste. And foolishness. And childishness: I'm not ready for the test, so I won't go to school. No, sweetie ("sweetness," she ironically corrects herself: that's what that man, who's probably feeling shittier that she is right now, used to call her, but that doesn't matter anymore), you're not allowed to duck out, you deal with this properly, step by step, and then we'll find out what you're really made of. *Got that?*

Write down those words, I'll tattoo them on me, a rough, surly voice pipes up from within, a very different woman, cynical, with in-your-face street-smart mannerisms picked up "on the inside" somewhere, quite capable of knocking you off your feet with curses should the need arise: if a person in general (every one!) is one big prison, then up to now this bitch inside her has lived tucked away in the remotest cell, coming out rarely, only when things got especially bitter and tough, and even so mainly for show: *P-pisses me off*—she'd hiss at moments of irritation, shaking her head and calming herself with an acrid smile; or else, digesting the aftertaste of the latest put-down (of which there was an overabundance lately) she would relate to her friends, her eyes wide with anger: *Trying to make me a patsy—I don't think so!*—right palm slapping hard against the crook of her left elbow as a clenched fist flew up—in America the prison hag learned how to swear in English and was especially successful at rendering the word *"Shhiitt!"*—a hiss off the arched back of a cat, and also the contempt-laced *"Oh come-on, give me a break!"* with which she once lashed that man—all in all, it was with that man that this disheveled witch with strangely unhealthy glistening eyes and teeth and some invisible but suspected criminal past would periodically run out to center stage, boldly smashing the fragile vessels of unfulfilled dreams; that man would liberate her, call her forth from the remote jail cell—as soon as she heard, during their first fight, that brutal, fist-swinging intonation of his: *"You tell me—what the fuck did I come way out here for, I had enough of this same shit at home—up to here!"*—the bitch eagerly rushed out to intercept him, she recognized a worthy partner, it was only here that they were truly partners—and then there was no stopping her as she spread her wings in previously untasted freedom: *"I started working on a head yesterday,"* he would try telling a fellow sculptor in her presence, and the bitch would tear out ahead, dropping buttons and pins in the insuppressible excitement of verbal excretion: *"That's wonderful, dear, you do need a head—it can only help!"*—he'd turn a hue so dark it seemed as though ink rather than blood flooded his face, whispering into her ear, *"Stop fucking me up!"*—the witch, exhaling cigarette smoke, laughed heartily from deep inside as she felt at least slightly pleased about something for the first time in a while: *"Now, now, dear, where's your sense of humor?"*—*"I left it back in our old apartment,"* he'd mutter (they left that apartment, thank God, and it would be best if the owners could seal it up for about half a year, until the smell of plague had dispersed)—"*Well why don't you run back and get it,*" the witch grinned, "*I'll wait here.*"— "*I've turned in my key,*" he'd mutter again, thinking that with that he'd put the issue to rest, but he was mistaken: "*I was the one who turned in the key, you still have the duplicate,*" she shot back: the power and lightning speed of their fencing with clubs was not to be apprehended by an outsider; no, say what you may, but they made a good pair, that much can't be denied! And now, when the time has come for that bitch—cursed and abused, scorched by misfortunes to the core, with a converted-to-acetone-but-still-extant spirit of survival (*where* in God's name does it come from?)—to accede to the throne and assume full reign of the prison, taking responsibility for the further course of whatever life may still smolder in it, dispensing orders all over the place: that door—do not enter, and this trash—get it the hell out of here right now, and that section way over there—air it out, we're converting it into a museum, and who's this loser dragging her ass and slobbering up the place, get her out of my sight! (*That's wonderful, dear, you do need a head—it can only help!*)—that bitch (and bitch she is!) has abdicated, turned into a smear on some distant wall, neither hide nor hair, and in all the caverns of the now empty prison an entirely different voice sounds, shuttling back and forth with uneven step: pitter-patter-pitter—then silence, and throwing itself against the walls, the same place time and again, each time weaker, while a poor, unloved girl abandoned at a rail station wails, and wails, and wails, eager to take the hand of anyone who says to her, "I'm your daddy," except who's going to say that to a thirty-year-old broad—that's the girl that you yourself hate inside you, you've tried to keep her under lock and key since you were an adolescent, in the dimmest, furthest basement chamber, without bread or water, not letting her move a muscle—and still she somehow managed to survive and there's no shutting her up now—now, when it seems that there's no one left except for her, that there is no other you.

You're messed up, "sweetness." You are really messed up. You've hit the end of the line—three months now that tremor has not left your body; in the mornings when you wake up (and especially now, when you wake up alone), the first thing you feel is your racing heartbeat and there's no putting it down—at least now you're sleeping without pills, and those horrible attacks of dry heaving you'd get at night remind you of themselves perhaps only when you're brushing your teeth and accidentally shove the toothbrush too far in—a swift nauseous gag, a subconscious repressed memory of your own dumb submission to those immediate, from the very first time—initially aroused, passionate whispers but after several weeks merely dry admonishments: *"Take it in your mouth…Take it in deeper…More, come on!"*—a dry spoon scratches your throat, the philosopher once said—here it is, right here. In the beginning she would still try to come to some understanding, to explain that she too may have some preliminary requests, and not just "down there:" is there nothing other than my sex organs that interests you? And: if you had plans for tonight, you might have let me know before I went to bed rather than sitting there scratching away at your engraving, and anyway,

you know I don't like to get undressed by myself...Okay—he
cheerily promised—we'll whip up such a grand overture for
you tomorrow!—tomorrow, however, never did come. Come
here—but I just took my sleeping pills—so, great, you'll
fall asleep with "him" inside you. God, what a nightmare
it was. How is it even possible to comprehend the world of
those who contemplate their own sex organ in the third
person? When they say to you, and that's the only way that
man said it—"Open 'her' up," all your senses are immediately transported to the gynecologist's stirrups—because
it's not *"she,"* it's *you* that's opening up—or in this case,
rather, locking down with a dead bolt. *You know how many
women I've had!—and not once was it bad, just plain bad!* Sure,
not for you, but what about them, ever think of asking? I
also never imagined things could be like this—but just *how*
bad it is, sweetheart, if you only knew. *Did you just bite me,*
he asked, fixing you with a strange, glassy stare, as on one
of your first nights, after lovemaking, he sat smoking at the
foot of the bed, *what is this*—meanwhile you were sprawled
back on the pillow giggling and feeling safe and stroking
his head with your outstretched foot, you had lovely legs,
all the Dior–St. Laurent models on their spikes would have
to run out and drown themselves immediately at the sight
of legs like that; it's only now that you've been wearing
pants for two months because your calves are decorated
like a map of an archipelago of multicolored, reddish and
brownish, peeled and peeling spots—scars, cuts, burns,
a visual manifestation of your nine-month (that's right,
nine months!!!) "mad love," from which you emerged as
madness itself, but back then you were simply stroking his
head with your foot, overcome with tenderness, drooling

idiot, the rough masculine "hedgehog" haircut felt good as it prickled your foot—when he suddenly turned and deftly pinned your leg to the bed: *Ah-hahh? So you like to bite? And what if I like to set you on fire, what then?*—you saw the cigarette lighter pressed against the inside of your knee and, rather than freeze in terror—as you stared down the barrel of that first apprehension of a steady, inhuman, *somehow different*, malevolently and madly searching gaze, on the edge of a grin of bared incisors protruding steeply from the upper lip, from which you afterward always defended yourself with laughter—you were only mildly surprised, and not all that consciously either—it's strange to what extent his presence, like dynamite, silenced in you all the previously not-too-badly developed instincts of self-preservation, which all floated to the surface belly-up, while the river kept on convulsing, blast after blast.

No, the premonitions were there; premonitions never lead you astray, it's only the determined force of our will that muffles their voice, interferes with our hearing them. The very first evening, at the arts festival where it all began—it was then that he rushed toward you as though you were all he'd been waiting for, "Oksana, I'm Mykola K., perhaps I can show you the city, perhaps I can take you to the castle, I have a car"—it was a ten-minute walk to the fabled castle up quiet, cobbled streets planted with plump baroque churches on each side; small-town seducer, you thought to yourself suppressing a smile, provincial dandy in your narcissistic get-up—tiny white collar peeking out from the sweater, manicured nails (and he's a painter!), an appropriately faint whiff of cologne—a feral cat with a gray buzz cut and roguish green-eyed squint, a slightly worn, threadbare artist's charm, dry wrinkled smile, furrowed bags under the eyes—"*and you said*," he recalled later, when you had entered the phase of creating the common mythology that no couple can do without (together with the legend about the Golden Age of their love with its own petty customs and rituals), the phase ended as quickly as it began—"*you said, hit the road, Jack*"—well, maybe not like that, or rather not exactly like that, but you showed no interest, that much is true—so it was all the more strange when on the evening of that same day you were visited by a glimpse of clear, ***penetrating insight***, which, it would be a crime to say otherwise, has never stood you up in a tight spot, but you tried to smother it, didn't you, many times, many! That evening, when the program was in full swing and you descended into the thick vapors of sweat and alcohol after reading your piece—two poems, two damned good poems projected straight into the intoxicated din of splotchy yellow faces congealed into one encompassing mass of flashing lights, or, more precisely, projected straight over it—holding on to the sound of your own, oblivious-to-all-around-and-subservient-only-to-words voice, a public orgasm, that's what you call this, but it does it for the crowd—every time and every place, even when they have no clue what the words mean, even in a foreign-speaking environment. You first discovered this at a writers' forum in one Far Eastern country where out of politeness they asked you to read in your native language ("you mean, it's not Russian?")—and you began reading then, in insult and desperation listening only to your own text (you were sick to death of their "Russian" even then), concealing yourself within it the way one slips into a lit house at night and locks the door behind, and midway you suddenly realized that in the frozen silence you were being heard: *mova*—your language, even though nobody understood it, in full view of the public it had concentrated around you into a clear, sparkling sphere of the most refined, crafted glass inside which magic was happening, this could be seen by all: something was coming to life, pulsating, firming up, arching into broad billows of flame—and then misting up again, as happens with glass that is exposed to heavy breathing; you finished your piece—enveloped, crystal-clear, protected, now that would have been the time to realize that your home is *your language*, a language only about a few hundred other people in the whole world can still speak properly—it would always be with you, like a snail's shell, and there would not be another, non-portable home for you, girl, ever, no matter what you do. And afterward all those peo-ple—round-faced, balding, dark- and curly-haired, with turbans and without—shook your hand long and with feel-ing and not letting you, incidentally, get to the bathroom (your stomach was giving a decided thumbs-down to their musky-spicy cuisine and was trumpeting, the bastard, precisely at the moments when gracious thank-yous were called for)—after that there was no audience you couldn't handle, even hardened criminals!—whether you call it exhibitionism or not, it was your own text that would always protect you from abuse and humiliation, you read it the way you wrote it—out loud, led by the self-propelling music of the verse, one normally does not allow witnesses to this process except in the theater, and that's why, in fact, it's so powerful. And that festival rabble, too, piped down somewhere in the middle of your reading—it surrounded the glass sphere and breathed in unison, and then when you, cooling off from the applause, were no longer on the platform but down below in the half-darkness in some tight, friendly circle: it's humid, smoky, someone was pouring a glass, someone was laughing, faces flashed by like film frames—you were stretching out your hand to get either a cigarette or a wineglass, that man appeared beside you for an instant as though he'd tripped over you accidentally, cat-eyes gleaming in the dark and excited whiskey-breath whisper: "You were great!"—and, equally casually, without pausing, he tried to squeeze your hand, reaching for it as it stretched toward the cigarette (or wineglass)—and you remembered this because (after all, who *didn't* shake your hand in that teeming multitude!) with that awkward grasp, that perpendicular chop across the thrust of your own arm, the same way he later raced up a one-way street the wrong way and got the police sirens after him, he managed to bend your thumb back in a particularly painful way, and your sirens also instantly started screaming—a lightning-quick flash through your consciousness—strange, how in that confused moment the message was so clear and you knew, as if some bystander in your head uttered a calm, meaningful, grammatical sentence: *"This man is going to hurt you."*

Precisely in this way, in other words, it was not the hurt thumb that was at issue, and you understood that perfectly. And that's the point, my dear—you knew everything right from the start; no, you knew it even before the start: about a week before that trip to the festival there was one evening when your bared nerve ends, painfully-thirstily, as only happens in the fall, exposed to the outside world—out to meet its faltering autumn colors and mysterious rustle in sleepy leaves—captured this passage, which you didn't grasp then and so left it unfinished:

Something has shifted in the world:
  someone was crying
Out my name in the night as though
  from a torture chamber
And someone rustled leaves on the porch,
Tossed and turned, and could not fall asleep.
I was learning the lessons of parting:
The science of differentiating the pain of illness
And the pain of affirmation (someone
  was writing me letters
And throwing them into the fire,
Unable to finish the line). Someone was waiting
For something from me, but I was silent:
I was learning the lessons of parting

—and now it has all come to pass, down to the very last word: go ahead, learn, learn now the lessons of parting— with life, with yourself, with your ill-fated gift, because it's unlikely that you'll now be able to raise it up—you've never yet managed to raise this barbell to full extension anyway.
    Ah, damn it all…

No, I would really like for someone to explain to me: *why the hell* would one come into this world a woman (and in Ukraine, yet!)—with this fucking *dependency* programmed into your body like a delayed-action bomb, with this crazi-ness, this need to be transformed into moist, squishy clay kneaded into the earth's surface (always, always liked the bottom position—sex from below, flat on your back: only then could she be eliminated completely, merging with the rhythm of her own body cells and the translucent pulsation of universal expanses—nothing even remotely like that ever happened with that man; at the moment when it seemed that she was just about to take off, he, without stopping, would awaken her from above with the harshly exhaled: *"Hmm-yeah, you'd need an infantry platoon to finish this job!"*—she had found this funny, but no more than that: *"What kind of talk is that?"*—she'd be offended: not at the words but at their detached tone—*"Silly, it's a compliment!—you should really consider trying it with two guys, you know what kind of rush you'd get?"*—it's quite possible that she might, she did, after all, like to bite during lovemaking, to suck hard at either a finger or a shoulder, to inhale a kiss until it made her head spin, a temple whore—that's who I must have been in my previous life, but in this life—in this, my dear, it is so much *not* all the same to me who I'm with: I remember sitting on a New York subway once, my head stuck in Toni Morrison's latest novel, and someone flopped down on the seat next to me pressing my whole body to the metal bar—and instantly I was electrified with a pure charge [like a high musical note] of such a powerful erotic urge that my body responded with an aroused swell, all buds bursting open inside like a tree in springtime: simultaneously I realized that this man had been hovering over me for a few subway stops already and had we not been people we'd already be fucking on this spattered floor, lovemaking for real, fusing not with your partner, no—with that wild, anonymous force that penetrates all living things with its current, you plug into it in order to, if only for a moment—aahhh!—catapult into the fiery-contoured darkness that has no name, no limit, on which all pagan cults lay their foundations, it's only Christianity that has classified this as union with the kingdom of the black god, sealing all exits for humans except for one—through the top, though not for our age, already essentially post-Christian, already cut off from the path of return back to the orgiastic feast of universal unity: we, each on his or her own, hopelessly infected with a cursed consciousness of the heaviness and density of his or her ego, and that is why the victoriously pure, loud, and high musical note broke off and extinguished itself in my body at the very moment that he, the one on my left, *began talking*: he spoke up after about one subway stop, some kind of uncivilized accent, asked what I was reading: am I in school or something, a student?—that's when I first *looked* at him, he was a young man in his late twenties, not tall but compactly built, a "Hispanic" hewed from a single block of wood, his gorgeous eyes the color of dark plums softened by a sensuous grayish mist, that's the way hundreds of men of different nations and skin colors have looked at me, each one from behind the bars of its own life, one can get out for a while, but not for good; "Pardon me?" I asked with that deliberately sharp voice one uses to dispense with insolents, and that Juan or Pablo or Pedro immediately realized that—it's over, the line's been cut—"Nothing," he blurted and continued to mumble something under his nose, now in his own language—the powerful animal voice of his body wilted, contracted, quickly-quickly went out, and beside me sat an ordinary immigrant lech—and anyway, he soon got up and headed either for the exit or elsewhere, I was no longer looking and back to reading to my book: the *person*, having peered out, broke the spell of the *sex*. Perhaps, really, the only way out of this prison is to go out at night, hiding your face deep in the hood of your coat, to get into strangers' cars without giving your name, the hand of the driver on your knee, a low, husky chuckle, a feverish rustle of excess clothing, no need to turn on the lights, just listen to the rumble of your blood, the male percussion part and your no-longer-your-own dissolving, dispersing, spreading, *ah, you've opened up so nicely*, yes! yes! more! more!—it's just that they all want to *talk*, splattering saliva and sperm they want a gulp of *you*: what are you reading, where are you going, are you married, you have to dream up a story—What's your name?—Irina—there was one incident when after locking into a strong deep steely kiss in an apartment entryway she slipped out and ran away, chuckling to herself, they all need to *vanquish*, that's the point, the give and take of a fair exchange like carbon dioxide–chlorophyll–oxygen is not for them, they don't know how to do it, and that man who's about to croak somewhere out there in the Pennsylvania wilderness currying favor with his diaspora blood brothers without a penny to his name or a word of English [which he was supposed to have studied up a little before coming, moron!]—boy, did he ever jump up, did he ever jerk his face up like a damned horse that's just been lashed when you finally sat him down in the coffee shop and, summoning all your fortitude to your aid, tried to introduce at least some kind of therapeutic clarity into your mutual physical and mental sickness—yes, everything you say is true, dear, and the fact that I no longer love you is also true: "*So you—what,*" the click of a jackknife blade popping up: "*feel like a 'victor' here, that you've won?*"—I think you just sat there with your mouth wide open: Mykola, you think we've been playing tug-of-war?..."*You know,*" again that steady ominous stare as though *something else* was peering through those eyes, rimmed by swollen red eyelids, like through the slits of a mask, "*if you were a man, I'd smash your face in!*" Very charming of you, dear—I, too, oh so often regret that I'm not a man).

> You're a woman. And that's your limit.
> Your moon sleeps like a silver fish lure.
> Like spices off the edge of a knife
> Dependency sprinkled into your blood

—so she murmured to herself during those frightening winter months, frightening in a different way from these-here autumn months: the middle of January, February, March—no news and no way of finding anything out between Cambridge—and a small Ukrainian provincial town, a studio heated by firewood in the attic of an abandoned house without an address or telephone, without a toilet or hot water, with only a bare lightbulb strung with a cord from the ceiling, with a stick of sausage and a jar of instant coffee on a low table greased with paint, *would you like a sandwich? oh, and I've got a tomato here, too, would you like some?* My God, the man lives like a stray dog, stays up until six in the morning checking out the window on that fancy automobile of his (sans garage) from behind the easel, at twenty-five or thirty you can still handle that kind of life, driven by sheer animal energy—but at forty! Meanwhile back at the Cambridge apartment, crisscrossed God knows how many times from one end to the other by senseless pacing—from the main door through the bedroom to the kitchen (the work that she purportedly came to the States to do collapsed like a crudely assembled house of cards)—something incomprehensible was happening with the phone: time after time she was awakened at dawn by random calls, she'd jump up and rush for the receiver: "Hello!"—somewhere in the distance on the voiceless line a wind howled and an ocean roared, for a few seconds the uninhabited, unpopulated space over the northern hemisphere announced itself as if in fact "someone was crying out her name at night as though from a torture chamber," and the cries did him no good, after which the mute signal would cease: the eyes of the buttons on the receiver lit up with a green, underwater glitter and from its mouth bubbled up a soulless dial tone—ah, you both had enough will to screw up all the phone lines over the Atlantic, that fierce, hungry force stormed out from his paintings and from your poems, you recognized his at once as soon as you ended up in his studio, put on your thick glasses, and stood before his canvases, and likewise he must have recognized yours—yours, which during those winter months was so unexpectedly and totally knocked off its newly discovered axis (because you were a woman, and a woman, damn it, is a climbing plant that without a vertical support, even if it is imagined—without a love with a concrete living face to it—falls to the ground and wilts, losing all inspiration for upward momentum: every poem was a delightful bastard baby of one prince or another with a bright star on his forehead, the star, of course, inevitably went out, the poem remained)—abandoned on its own, that force tore you to bits from within, fiercely scratching at the walls of your being and bursting out in desperate freefall—

And suddenly again I wanted to scream
Howl at the lamp, claw at the
Wallpaper—from the reality of loss
From knowing there's no purpose to waiting for you

—until one March day your whole insides were scalded by a frightening thought: that he's dead, that he just "hit the wall" the way he wanted to (he confessed this to her practically at the beginning—smiling a crooked smile as he hit the gas, racing the car like a plane on the runway, on a country road in the middle of the night, and the wet streetlights in the fine-needled silvery frames, and the black olive flash of the approaching puddles—everything merged, rushed forward in a race against itself, taking your breath away, one hundred, one twenty, one forty, one... one hundred and sixty?—*you're not afraid? don't you get the desire to*—*hit the wall?*—no, I'm not afraid, I never really experienced real fear and truthfully, I don't feel it even now—strange, incomprehensible actually, especially if you take into account my whole, damn it to hell, slave-gang life, no wonder it began with a clinical death at birth, Mother even recalled a piece of feces hanging from my bottom, and the tiny body had already turned blue: the poor soul poked its head out into the world and lost its nerve—Hey, no way, let me go back!—but thanks to some kind folks it was revived, quite quickly really, no need to snivel, there are things scarier than death, I know them, it's just that *that* fear—seductive and dark, the bewitching, intoxicating excitement of *perdition* that lives inside him, and I've discerned it in others, too—that I don't have, period, that's why he would look at me with that spark of unconcealed excitement in his eye, even when it was all over: "*You're a brave woman!*"—and that "wall" jumped past me then without scaring me)—but this thought—that he died, that those mysterious phone calls really were from him: from "the other side," and that means then that her love did not protect him, that she herself, she herself, narcissistic egotistical bitch with her stupid pride, her cheap pomp, her empty strutting had pushed him toward that "wall"—a princess, no less: oh, so that's how it is? Fine, then I'm off—America, as everyone knows, is "the land of opportunities," half of Europe, and not just our godforsaken part but the purest, from Britain to Italy, is dying to get over there, money, career ("Music, women, champagne..." he had ironically echoed then), and what is there in Ukraine, Ukraine is Chronos chomping away at his children, tiny fingers and toes, I'm supposed to sit and wait for what, to suck a frog's tit, or rather that of a menopausal diaspora gramps—the Antonovych prize? Oh my God, **what** the fuck is all that to me if he's dead, what, what, what has happened to him?!—the thought was so unbearable that jumping out to the back porch and raising her face to the mutable, rapidly darkening Cambridge sky that was thickening into a cloudy gouache, opening her lungs, sticky from motionless sitting and cigarette smoke, to catch the barely felt ocean breeze, she started to pray—yes, the way she had only prayed twice before in her life, once for her father, who was spending his last days lying in a hospital after the by-then-unnecessary operation, convulsing for hours from the metasthasis-induced stabs of pain (they had not yet put him on the narcotics)—for God to send him a speedy end, and then a second time, embarrasing to recall—for independence, then, on the twenty-fourth of August 1991, when everything was decided in hours, as generally happens in the lives of people and nations: Lord, she begged, trembling—help—not for our sakes for we are unworthy, but for all those who have died before us in this cause, of whom there is no count—and both prayers were heard, prayers *like that* always reach their addressee; and here now she was begging: Lord, please make him be alive!—he can forget me, he can return to his wife, he can betray me with whomever he wishes, I don't have to have him for my husband, and I don't need anything at all from him, and if it is your will, Lord, I will love another, I'll have children with another, just—O Lord, let him be alive. And healthy. And happy. Only that, Lord. Only that.

Well, "healthy and happy"—that would be kind of pushing it, sweetness, because not even God can force somebody to be happy, so the final version of your desperate telegram had to have been accepted without those two words—it's not like God is going to take orders from every fool! (And I wonder, how do they run this business up there—is there an angel-secretary selecting these earthly messages as they come in, retrieving the *sincere* ones from the stream, the hot and the heavy, and calmly dropping the incalculable

masses of *empty* words into a black hole?—poems work
pretty much the same way: you're disgusted as soon as you
feel the empty sort coming out, you drop the poem without
finishing.) And there was one other point where you lied—
"he can forget me," you babbled half-consciously, knowing
firmly all the while that never will he forget you, not now,
not for as long as he lives: pinching a cigarette butt between
finger and thumb and flicking it backwards so that it lit
up an arc through the air: *"And have you considered how long
it's going to take me to get over you? Huh?"* he hissed, barely
holding himself back from hurling her after the cigarette
butt (*"Keep in mind, the flesh is weak, I could hack you to bits
before I know it,"* he had once confessed, and your lightbulb
went on: watch this, watch this! he's not lying, this is the
truth!—and, with an instantly switched on *impersonal* interest—invisible wires hummed, droned, nimbly transmitting
information—you squeezed it out of him that time, despite
his iron-clad resistance to all kinds of cuddly, mumbly,
purring, come-on-tell-me boobie interrogations—a taut,
point-form account of how, a long time ago, when he was
decorating a church together with a *"fucker who was really
getting to me,"* he got into a state where he was chasing the
fellow around the grounds axe-in-hand—really, around
the church, you wondered, somehow imagining that this
must have taken place in the dead of night, because there
is nothing more frightening than a church at night with
a full moon reflected in the dark windows high above—
and it's since then that he's always been on guard, ready
to run at the first sign of *that* particular mood coming
on—*I see*, you hm-ed, *interesting*, although the only thing
interesting about it was the total absence of fear on your

part, dope—it's as if it were all being told to you through a window in the visiting room of a prison or an insane asylum: you hear it out, and then you leave, and behind you the leaden doors screak violently as they close shut, as the dry clicking of the key turning in the lock showers your back, injecting itself under your skin). How long will it take me to get over you, how long for you to get over me, "How much longer are we to walk thus, Father?" asked the wife of the defrocked Avvakum trudging behind him, outcast and banished, across the endless plain, and sitting down on a hillock, exhausted by the pointlessness of the trip, she heard in reply: "Until death, Mother." Eastern fatalism, oh yes—the Russians have it; we're in worse shape, we, actually, are neither here nor there, Europe has managed to infect us with the raving fever of individual desire, faith in our personal "Yes I can!"—however, we never developed a foundation for such faith, those structures that might support that "I can!" and thus have tussled about for ages at the bottom of history—our Ukrainian "I can!" helpless and alone. Amen.

What is it that made you think that *you can* pull him out of that hole into which he (it was obvious!) was so determined to sink? Actually, you should have taken heed on the first night—when, still undressing, he squinted attentively, as if determining a price: *"Can you come before I do?"*—you laughed, overflowing with frothy confidence like a bottle of young wine: *"I can do anything!"* Fool, you should have seen right there that he was *no partner* for you, that, petrified inside from years of permafrost, he was simply incapable of being not alone—even in lovemaking (*"You're such a good fuck!"* was all he could squeeze out of himself after a long and cumbersome back-and-forth, after tortured convulsions, after all those pathetic lamentations—*"Oh, why did I drink so much!"* and *"Ah, damn, I wanted you so badly!"*—after falling into a momentary sleep, a solitary sleep, deadly removed from her presence beside him: he never moved once as she strained to extricate herself from his embraces, so fuck you, you miserable impotent, I'll get up, get dressed, make some coffee, the buses will start running soon, and I'll get back to the hotel, in the windows of the studio the blue tint of dawn grew inescapably paler, more watery, contours of angular piles of canvases stacked up against the walls emerged from the quivering protoplasmic twilight, a terrible hour, hour of the ill and the forty-year-olds, it is probably in this kind of gray murkiness that dead souls are tormented—that's when he woke up and hurt her, hurt her for real, forget the pain of losing your virginity, *painful intercourse*, that's how the phenomenon is defined in the medical literature which she, the browbeaten Soviet dolt, began studying only in America, she even went to see the doctor, swallowing utter humiliation, to find out whether there wasn't something, Dear God, wrong with her sexually, and bugged out her eyes in disbelief when the doctor shrugged her shoulders, "I don't see any problems"—but back then, as she shrieked wildly and jerked back, kicking out her legs [her battered uterus ached a full twenty-four hours afterward, like bad menstrual cramps]—*"You're hurting me, you're hurting me, you hear me?"*— she also felt, over his fierce and victorious cry: *"And how about marrying me? And how about having my child? You silly girl, can't you see I love you?"*—his moist, swollen hotness kindling and distending inside her, yes, this moment is everything—and for its sake stay, oh please stay a bit longer, don't go, deep sighs, he emerges from her with so many years washed away from his face, smoothed with a moist sheen of happiness, her own eyes misted over by involuntary tears of tenderness and in those tears his thin, sharp features, pointed ears and cheekbones of a postwar village urchin [father liberated from a Nazi POW camp and off to the Gulag, mother working the beetfields on the collective farm] standing in the pasture with a stick in his hand, dumbstuck for the first time by the crimson gold swirling over the horizon as far as the eye can see amid smoky-gray clumps of clouds, the world was on fire, ever-changing, all this was in his paintings, oh to free that lad from this taciturn, thin-lipped, carefully groomed and clean-shaven man—"*You've never given birth? Your lips smell of fresh milk—I'll give you a child, you hear? A little boy*"—that in itself was a completely satisfying work of art in which your personal physical dissatisfaction did not weigh all that heavily—left alone, because he, wrapping himself into a long-flapped robe resembling a trench coat took off right away to wash up: the ritual of an asshole, if you stop to think about it, but even that didn't particularly jar you then—you purred and stretched, cracking your entwined arms over you head and admitted to yourself with a raspy giggle—well, you've finally been properly *fucked*, girlfriend, uncensored version—properly fucked for the first time in your life, because until now it was more like a service, aimed to please, fussed over you like over warm dough, asked what kind of words you liked to hear in bed, but here someone just took you and screwed the living daylights out of you like a thug, no dither—and strangely, this thought, too,

was not unpleasant, and when you pulled your compact out
of your purse frightened of what you'd see in there—after
three nights of no sleep, countless cigarettes and midnight
cognacs, very successful arts festival!—you found yourself
flushed with pleasant surprise: a clear, suddenly youthful
and doing justice to your authentic beauty, delicate, thin,
almost childish face peered out at you, dark eyes darting
out ahead, a face you always knew was in there somewhere
but hadn't seen in the mirror in God knows how long: you
had come home, you were *home*—and he sat at the foot of
the bed, smoking and watching, his luminously enchanted
face, riveted on you, lit up the still dim studio—occasionally
he would lean over you gently, concealing a smile, in order
to kiss your nipples poking up from under the rolled-back
plaid blanket, and to carefully, slowly wrap you up to your
neck again, like a peasant tending to his property, and to
bring you a cup of coffee, "*be careful not to spill any,*" and you
immediately spilled some as you shook with laughter, "*I'll
put this plaid out on display with a sign saying who splattered it,*"
and unexpectedly his "*Why were you crying?*"—I won't tell, I
won't tell you yet, I'll tell you in time, and once said, I'll be
repeating it almost every minute: in the absence of any other,
more potent words—when there's no cistern large enough
to scoop out the bottomless well, one is left to lower and
raise the same childish pail over and over—the monotony
of repetition, the creak of the crank: I love you. I love you.
I love you).

So there it was, girlfriend—you fell in love. And how you
fell in love—you exploded blindly, went flying headfirst,

your witch's laugh ringing to the heavens, lifted by the invisible absolute power of whirlwinds, and that pain didn't stop you—although it should have—but no, you cut the juice to all your warning signs that had lit up with all their red lights flashing and screamed "meltdown"—like before the accident at the atomic station—and only your poems, which switched on immediately and rushed forward in a steady, unrelenting stream, sent out unambiguous signals of danger: persistent flashes of—hell, and death, and sickness,

And the yellow sea of days, and
   the gray sea of dreams
In the reflected colors of the dying sky—
And I'm still swimming—but you've hit bottom
And it's frightening for both of us to watch ourselves.

"In other words, you knew?" he snapped, lighting that wolf-ish glare in his eye, when she—there was nothing to lose anymore, gathered the courage to read him some of that poetic stream aloud—*"you knew this would happen? So why the hell?..."* Uh-huhh, my dear, that's the point...

N-nope, you weren't a masochist, you were a fucking normal woman whose body took pleasure in giving joy to others, what can I tell you—you were a cool broad, "sweet baby," "phenomenal lady," "stud woman," mull it over and over again in your head now, this guest-comment (commendation) book—made up of those moments when men don't lie, maybe you'll get a drib of balance back into your life: it did happen! after all—but no, it's not coming back to save you—so what, if it's true, if you always felt, sometimes with more, sometimes with less dark residue of unfulfillment, how much better you still *could* be—because there are things in life independent of us, because I am as you are with me—it's a little different with men, but for women, unfortunately, that's how it is—and, unfortunately, in all things; and no matter how many bras are burned by American feminists, masturbation—whether with a rubber penis or a living person, because with a living person it's also no more than masturbation if it's without love—will give you neither poems nor children. And that's it, period. "That's you limit." How was it that Cambridge poem ended?

> A field that yearns for the harrow,
> And the wet, tearstained ravens—
> And the man, who could not protect—
> But wanted me to protect him.

Yep, exactly, or *bien sûr*, if you prefer. Yet another reason why this foreign country is doing you no good—it's clogging up your brain, your nose, with the lint, down, and powder of foreign words and phrases, clogging all the pores and rudely shoving them into your hand even when you're alone with yourself, and before you realize it, you're beginning to speak "half this, half that," in other words, the same thing that happens at home (home? get a grip, woman—where is this place, your home?), fine, okay, I mean in Kyiv, in Ukraine—with the Russian: it seeps in from the outside in tiny droplets, becomes dried and cemented, and you are obligated—to either continuously conduct a cleansing, synchronic translation in your head, which sounds forced and unnatural—or else to role-play, like we all do, using your voice to take the foreign words into quotation marks, place a kind of clownish-ironic stress on them like they were a citation (a good example for students in tomorrow's class, for instance, would be "*So you—what, feel like a 'victor' here, that you've won?*").

And you also might say—appearing with a lecture at some American university, or at the "triple-A, double-S" conference, or at the Kennan Institute in Washington, or wherever else the ill wind blows you, an honorarium of a hundred, two hundred bucks max, plus travel costs—and thank you very much, you're not Yevtushenko or Tatiana Tolstaya to get thousands for each appearance, and who the hell are you anyway, backwater Ukrainian from the Khrushchev communal housing projects that you've been trying to break out of your whole damn life to no avail, Cinderella who crosses the ocean to grouse over dinner at Sheffield's with a pair Nobel prize winners (radiating in all directions, juggling four languages at once across the table) about the intellectual bankruptcy of contemporary civilization, after which you return to your six-square-meter Kyiv kitchen to fight with your mother and be humiliated by having to explain to various editors that "my homeland will be where I am" does not at all mean *ubi bene, ibi patria*— not least because with this fucking patria it will never and nowhere be *bene* for you, neither at Sheffield's, nor at Tiffany's, nor in Hawaii, nor Florida—because your home- land is not simply the land of your birth, a true homeland is the country that can *kill* you—even at a distance, the same way a mother slowly but inexorably kills an adult child by holding it near, shackling its every move and thought with her burdensome presence—ah, to make a long story short, the topic of my lecture today, ladies and gentlemen, is, as noted in the program, "Fieldwork in Ukrainian Sex," and before I begin I would like to thank all of you, present here and absent, for the completely unjustified attention you have given my country and my humble persona—because if there's one thing that we haven't been spoiled by yet it's attention: to put it bluntly, we've been lying there dying, unnoticed by bloody anybody (and I'm still in a rather privileged position here, because if I were to really have the guts to say fuck it and pour the rest of those tablets in the orange bottle down my throat, my body would be found relatively soon, I'd say, probably within three days: Chris, the departmental secretary, will call if I don't show up for class, therefore, it would be a crime to complain, the spider web–thin thread, slight as it is, still hangs there and I could pull on it to let the world know about my next, this time my final, departure, I do have it—and if something were to happen with that man in the Pennsylvania wilderness—although I really doubt that anything should happen to him, he'd never do it himself, too much rage for this kind of business—then he's got Mark and Rosie checking in on him daily)—so, ladies and gentlemen, please do not be in a hurry to qualify the presented case of love here as pathological, because the speaker has not yet stated what is most important—the main point, ladies and gentlemen, lies in the fact that in the research subject's life this was her first *Ukrainian* man. Honestly—the first.

The first one *ready-made*—whom she did *not* have to teach Ukrainian, to drag book after book from her personal library out on dates with him just to broaden the common internal space on which to build a relationship (Lypynsky, Hrushevsky, and he hadn't heard of Horska either, nor Svitlychny, his idea of the 1960s dissident movement was completely different, good, I'll bring it for you tomorrow!), or if in bed after lovemaking you inadvertently quote "nor dreams' abode—the sacred home," you have to immediately launch into a half-hour commentary on the life and works of the author—oh, there was this writer in Western Ukraine in the 1930s—and that's the way it was your whole damned life!—professional Ukrainianizer, like growing a whole new organ for each of them, and if some day our independent, or rather not-yet-dead country, if it doesn't die by then, should institute some special award—for the highest number of Ukrainianized bed spaces, you'd surely sock it to them with your grand list of conversions!—but this was the first man from *your world*, the first with whom you could exchange not merely words, but simultaneously the entire boundlessness of shimmering secret treasure troves, reflections from inside the deepest wells that are revealed by those words, and therefore it was as easy to talk as to breathe and to dream, and that's why the conversation was drunk eagerly with parched, dry lips, the intoxication ever more dizzying, ah, this never-before experienced total freedom to be yourself, this four-hands piano playing, at last, across the entire keyboard, inspiration and improvisation, so many sparks, laughter, and energy suddenly released, when each note—ironic hint, nuance, wit, touch—resonates at once, picked up by your interlocutor, somersaults in the air for no reason other than excess of strength, a casual touch of the knee—a little closer: may I? and now a little more ambiguous, more risky, and now—up close and personal, and finally, turning off the car engine (because you did end up getting into that stupid car of his after all—after visiting his studio, after you saw with your own eyes *who* he was)—an abrupt switch to a different language: lips, tongue, hands—and you, leaning back with a moan, *"Let's go to your place...To the studio..."*—a language that drastically shortened your path toward one another, you recognized him: he's one of yours, yours—in everything, a beast of the same species!—and in that language there was everything, everything of which there would later be nothing between you in bed.

"Gosh, if only he weren't such a damned good painter!" you were saying, sitting in a bar called Christopher's in Porter Square, you had drunk two glasses of cabernet sauvignon on an empty stomach and it relaxed you a little—for the first time in all those Cambridge months, giving you a lightheaded audacious uplift, "bottle of wine, fruit of the vine..." ah, too bad nobody to break into song with—Lisa and Dave sat listening like children being told a Christmas story, forgetting all about crunching their chips, "Slavic charm," that's what they would call it—you used to like that bar, the dull bottle-green of the décor that would bring card tables to mind, and also the low-hanging lights that drew faces into the shadows, and the men crowding the bar watching the baseball game, and the din of voices, the night outside the distant windows, its thick, brown murkiness melting the candy-yellow street lamps—everything at once, because only thus can you enter an *alien* world: accepting everything at once, with all your senses, and you know how to do that, you had simply grown tired, after all these years of homeless wandering, of loving the world *all alone*—of passing, anonymous and unrecognized, through all the dusky airport terminals, the restaurants and bars with their warm lights, the sea-shores with their shuffle of incoming waves against the rough sand, the early-morning hotels with coffee in the lobby—"Where are you from?"—"Ukraine."—"Where's that?"—you had grown tired of *not being* in this world, tired of dragging home in your teeth the bundles of beauty that you had thirstily sucked in from it and shout-ing happily: "Hey, come see!"—but at home, in your poor beaten-down country, a country of government officials with sagging pants and generous sprinkles of dandruff on their jackets, greasy writers adept at reading in one language only and not partaking of that ability all too often, and shifty-eyed, cockroach-like businessmen with the habits of former Komsomol organizers—none of this seemed to fit in anywhere, it just hung there aimlessly and was only capable of irritating up to inducing an attack of bile with its foggy, coded inaccessibilty of unfamiliar names and customs, its fat, homegrown, self-taught dilet-tantes (and for some reason inevitably on short, bowed legs, like jockeys: a special breed or something?) pickled somewhere in a provincial public library bearing a for-saken commissar's name, and here you had the gall (or perhaps dumb blind luck, they thought?) to hang out at

Harvard's Widener Library or wherever else—you had grown tired of the inability to *share* your love for the world and in that man—as soon as you stepped into his studio and stood (donning your thick glasses) before the canvas upon canvas facing you, propped up against the walls gathering dust, you knew at once that you had found your only, one-hundred-percent-assured chance *not to be alone* in that love—precisely because he was "such a damned good painter"—but this much it was hopeless to explain to Lisa and Dave, and you didn't even try, Lisa was smiling, moved, with her unrealistically bright mouth looking like an aroused coral mollusk, her eyes shining mistily: "What a story!" Oh, yes, a terribly romantic love story—with fires and car accidents (because one night he went out and crashed that celebrated car of his, totaled it, as he told her), with the mysterious disappearance of the protagonist and the departure of the heroine across the ocean, with piles of poems and paintings, and mainly—with this persistent irrational omnipresent feeling that ultimately seduced you: the feeling that *everything is possible*: the man played without rules, or rather, he played by his own rules like a true Kantian genius, and in his magnetic field any kind of logical prediction of events was doomed to failure, thus he was his own "land of opportunities," and whatever there lay hidden for the future among those "opportunities"—death in the next of a series of auto accidents (no, God, only not that!) or a triumphal march through the museums of the world—it didn't matter, who the hell cares, as long as we can break out, tear ourselves away from the beaten track—from that eternal Ukrainian *curse of nonexistence.*

That's a separate topic, ladies and gentlemen, mesdames et messieurs, forgive me if I've taken up too much of your time, it's not easy for me to talk about all this, and I'm also actually quite seriously ill, my frightened, hungry, and if we're not going to bother with euphemisms then we could just say raped body has been unable, for the third month now, to curtail this light internal tremor, especially horrible—ad nauseam!—below the stomach where I continuously feel a pressing, beating quiver, and when I spread my fingers they immediately take on a life of their own, each marching to its own drummer as though they've been stretched and separated from each other, and I won't mention the puckered teenage pink pimples that have blossomed over my shoulders and face and there's nothing I can do about it—the wretched body is still alive, it's demanding its rights, it's dying from basic sex deprivation, perhaps it could even recover, start hopping around like a bunny rabbit if it could get sweetly laid, but, unfortunately, this problem is not so easy to solve; moreover if you're all alone in a country you don't know and a city you don't know, in an empty apartment where the phone rings only to offer—a rare opportunity, and this week only—a hu-u-uge discount on a subscription to the local newspaper, an apartment from which you dig yourself out three times a week to get to the university where half a dozen neatly dressed, white socks and sneakers, and fastidiously washed and deodorized American kids with moist, healthy skin and teeth follow you with their eyes as you wander back and forth across the classroom, the eyes of fish in an aquarium, quietly writing something down (God only knows what) in their notebooks while you, getting yourself all worked up (you have to hang in there somehow for an hour and fifteen minutes!), passionately explain to them that Gogol had no choice! given that he was who he was, no choice but to write in Russian! you can cry, you can dance—no choice! (and you likewise have no choice but to write in Ukrainian, although this is probably the most barren choice under the sun at present, because even if you did, by some miracle, produce something in this language "knocking out Geothe's *Faust*," as one well-known literary critic by the name of Joseph Stalin would put it, then it would only lie around the libraries unread, like an unloved woman, for who knows how many dozens of years until it began "cooling off"—because untasted, unused texts unsustained by the the energy of reciprocal thought gradually cool down, and how!—if the stream of public attention doesn't pick them up in time and carry them to the surface, they sink like stones to the bottom and become covered by mineral waxes that can never be scraped off, just like your unsold books which gather dust somewhere at home and in bookstores, this same thing has happened with most of Ukrainian literature, you can count on the fingers of two hands—not even authors, but individual works that have been lucky enough—with numb fingertips and tears in your eyes you had read a translation of *Forest Song* done here in America, an authorized version meant for the Broadway stage, you were as high as a kite from your quickened, passionate breathing: it's alive, alive, it hasn't perished, seventy years later, on a different continent, in a different language—just look at that, it made it!—of course, it's an entirely different matter to write in English or in Russian—your first poem published in

English in a not particularly well-known magazine received a rave review from somewhere out there, Kansas, I think, some kind of *Review of Literary Journals*, can you believe it, and Macmillan is ready to include it in its anthology of international women's poetry, "you're a superb poet," the local publishers tell you [dragging their feet on publication all the same], thank you, I know, so much the worse for me—but you, sweetness, you have no choice not because you're incapable of switching languages—you could do that splendidly with a little effort—but because a curse has been placed on you to be faithful to all those who have died, all those who could have switched languages just as easily as you—Russian, Polish, some even German, and could have lived entirely different lives, but instead hurled themselves like firelogs into the dying embers of the Ukrainian with nothing to fucking show for it but mangled destinies and unread books—and yet today there is you, unable to step over their corpses and go on your merry way, simply unable, tiny sparks of their presence keep dropping into your life here and there, into the ashes of mundane daily existence; and this then is your family, your family tree, you pitiful backwoods aristocrat, please forgive this unpardonably long digression, ladies and gentlemen, all the more because it actually has no relevance to our subject). Ladies and gentlemen, the sense of one's own body wasting away day by day—is a feeling familiar perhaps to prisoners of the Gulag: I examine myself in the bathroom every evening (putting on my owl's glasses, those same ones with the thick lenses, so I look pretty darn funny), my breasts, until now invariably round and bouncy with pert nipples pointing in opposite directions ("Check it out," one of my not yet fully Ukrainianized men once said, and not all that long ago—"they're probably a size D, but see how high they sit!"): this fall they sagged for the first time, definitively moving downward, bringing to mind bread dough that's been standing around too long, and they've also been attacked by some kind of revolting spots, probably pigmentary, and the nipples are looking more and more like the dark skin of a shriveled peach—that man was one of those who generally had a very foggy notion of what you're supposed to do with women's breasts except perhaps pinch them through a blouse, but the point, of course, isn't that—this was a good-looking body, healthy, smart, and vigorous, and to give credit where credit is due, it hung in there for an awfully long time, it was only with that man that it instantly began giving me a hard time, but I put the screws to it, harshly and unsparingly, and still it resisted, chafed with various chronic colds, swollen glands, and febrile rashes, a "weakened immune system," the doctors said, but I would pry myself out of bed, patch the rashes with plasters, and, burning with fever, charge to the train station, the train, clattering over the jointed tracks, would rush me toward the city in which that man sat silently after totaling his precious car, the night of the accident I had a dream that someone had stolen it from him, and verses, unaware of the real state of things but in their own way somnambulantly clairvoyant, flooded in like the landscapes from the fog outside the window:

> The snow, back then, was yet to fall.
> Autumn still smelled of Corvalol,
> And cars, run off the road,
> In their garages weakly groaned.

I abused my body for a fairly long time and it must have some sense of grievance against me (or, as they say here, "a grudge"), and now, after the fact, there's not a whole lot I can do for it—except torment it every morning with pointless knee-bends after which the tight, deceived thighs ache with forgotten, sweet moans; or else vapidly drag it to the swimming pool every night (off to work!) where they know me already: the black lady custodian in a motley turban who hands out locker keys blitzes me with her blinding smile each time: "You're pretty faithful to that swimming, huh?"—God, how gentle, soft, and kind she is, like the water in the pool; at each unexpected kind word I'm ready to start bawling my eyes out, like a hounded adolescent wolf cub, ready to eat from each outstretched hand, like, for example, this trustingly open palm—pink nakedness upward—handing me a little golden key on a red nylon string, to which I eagerly explain that I must, that I literally must frequent this place, that this is the sole way I can save myself from depression—the Great American Depression from which it seems that about 70 percent of the population suffers, running to psychiatrists, gulping down Prozac, each nation goes crazy in its own way—and in order to describe my depression, which actually falls under a different name—I've already managed, willy-nilly, to pick up a little terminology familiar to them: "broken relationship," and moreover "straight after a divorce," and moreover "sexually traumatic," and from there summoning psychiatric textbooks to my aid: "fear of intimacy, fear of frigidity, suicidal moods"—in a word, a classic case, not even worth going to a psychiatrist with, and my blessed African woman, so lusciously fleshy behind the narrow counter,

Earth Mother, gentle, steamy moos and rough tongue, nods with a wise, knowing smile: "I've been there," she says, "with the father of my kids"—how about that, so she's divorced, a single parent with two little ones, the younger will be two soon, it's easier when you have children—both easier and harder (*"And now,"* said that man, glowing triumphantly over her, a sweaty boy in the dark—*"and now you're going to be pregnant: I came right inside you!"*—*"No,"* she laughed, gently so as not to spill all that tenderness over the brim—*"no, my love, it won't be today"*—although this in fact was, from the first night, her main concealed thought, the submerged underwater current of that love: *a baby boy,* Danny, she secretly established—forehead covered in tickly baby-chick down, frog-like tiny legs tucked in, fingertips like the tiniest buds, oh, my Lordy!—in her dreams she eagerly cradled him to her breast: this is the anchor that keeps us alive and without which we, ladies, do not have full rights on this earth, "unregistered": neither a word nor even a letter in that text but merely an accidental dot in the margins—and in the meantime her verses mumbled mutely to themselves, dispersing into multiglossia:

I'm cold, my darling.
—Wrap a sheepskin around you
I'm sad, my love
—Try working, my dove
Ah, but I'm feeling lazy
—Because you need a baby
I'm frightened, my dear, to have her,
And thus become yours forever

—no, no, I mustn't think if it, I mustn't!)—"Everybody seems to have been there," I remark, feeling momentarily relieved of the heavy weight by joining at least some kind of community, a *social group*: join the club!—oh, yes, my black woman gives a stately nod, "every woman has been there"—and then a mischievous woman's squint: "maybe you'll meet someone here, at the pool?" That would have been the moment to start laughing hysterically, at the very least because this fall, as you forcibly dragged your miserable, oppressed body down the streets of an alien city, you first became familiar with the notion of *invisibility*—at first you didn't even quite realize what the deal was, but once you did, you began to study it fastidiously: yup, it's true— men walking toward you would glide over you with indifferent, unseeing eyes, like you were an inanimate object, and even on the bus, when pressed by the crowd into dangerously close proximity to somebody's massive back with a hockey emblem on it, you did not pick up that lightning-quick flash of animal instinct—a twitch, a face turning to look at you—that which switches on in them automatically, simply from the smell of a woman but not only: in reality they—perhaps only with the exception of camp prisoners and soldiers, those who have lost their minds after years of abstinence—respond not so much to the woman as to the electric frequencies, undetectable by any scientific instrument, of all the other males' desires which at the moment happen to be aimed at her and which envelop her (and which at the present moment do *not* envelop me) as a densely charged erotic cloud—no wonder they say a betrothed woman is attractive to all: that's the part that really seduces them, forces them to flare with nostrils

dilated by fury and pound the ground with their hooves—
the spirit of competition, the desire to win, the challenge
to a duel, the silent call of the bugle to battle that vibrates
the air, the insatiable need to prove superiority over all
others, doesn't matter if they've ever seen them or not: *"Tell
me—was sex with your husband good?"—"Very good!"*—she
blurted out truthfully, like a slap in the face—he practically
curled into a ball: too bad, she no longer had the strength
to force those patent phrases through her throat, to pretend, swallowing insult after insult, to brazenly demonstrate, like a whore for money, how very all-out cool he is
(*"You slut, dumping your tits out for all to see!"* he hissed as
though a bee had just bitten him when during their final
days of communal habitation he caught sight of her half-
naked body, angry at himself that he could still, against
all common sense, want this woman with whom sex was
nothing but mutual torment: *"your cunt's like a vice"*—well,
you shouldn't have gone in with a crowbar: hopping under
the covers at three in the morning, shoving me around,
turning me over on my back, that businesslike manner of
sticking your finger in where you're not invited, that much
I can do for myself and a whole lot better than you, more
gently; my body defended itself against my own willfulness,
oh yeah, *fear*, so thoughtlessly dismissed by me earlier,
appeared out of nowhere, planted itself inside my body
and grew: my body sensed *something* in this man that I could
not—meantime I turned myself into a witch, a castrating
Megaera with a vice in my loins: ever hear of "no"?!—and
that's when the bellowing of the trapped male would com-
mence: *"You know how many women I've had!"*—Oh fuck your
women, all one hundred thousand of them, I couldn't care

less, I don't need to conquer you, I need to love you—love, can you understand that?!—therefore in her nakedness, we must admit he had a point, there truly was a shamelessness: it was a deliberate and offensive nakedness, that which is not meant to seduce but rather to express contempt—I can cut my toenails in front of you, shave my legs, not rinse the bathtub after I'm done, leaving dark curly hairs on the sides, wash up between my legs, masturbate—and not in the same way as when each such expression of physical liberty is taken as a gift, as one more precious sign of trust that evokes in you a hot torrent of grateful tenderness, not the way it was between us back home during those days when we would meet in unexpected quarters, crawling into some friend's empty cottage through a window on a cold November night where the temperature was about seven degrees Celsius, drinking cognac in the dark, so as to warm up a little, without taking our coats off, and I was blowing into your rough, frozen hands and hiding them under my sweater because that was the warmest spot, and you both laughed and cried, catching your breath, not able to believe it: *"Is this you? Can this really be you?"*—that autumn was the autumn of keys; never in my life had I, homeless, carried around so many borrowed keys in my purse at the same time—it seemed as though I jangled with them as I ran, like a merry-go-round pony, attracting all eyes to me, which gave me, like that pony from the fair, an irrepressible desire to neigh happily—and when you, in that home that belonged to some unknown, were boiling water in two huge pots so that I could take a bath, drawing it by pail in the middle of the night from an invisible well in the yard, identifiable only by the occasional splash, while I hung around the doorway in nothing but a housecoat over my naked body feeling no cold; and later, when I locked the bathroom door and saw the soap still foamy after you in the soap dish, standing there gingerly on end the way you had a habit of carefully placing it—so that the water would drain, because mine was always flat on its belly soaking in a puddle—I stood looking at that soap and was so stupidly happy as I could only have been in my childhood, because only then had I had a home, I was tired, my love, I was so tired, and all I wanted was for you to be near me and to lather me up, but you locked me in that room and turned the key and took off somewhere into the night in that car looking for groceries—oh, God damn it, fuck those groceries, my good man, how much life do we really have and how much love that we should be slicing it neatly for breakfast and dinner!). *"How many times were you in love?"*—*"Three,"* he counted, shutting his eyes—*"this is the fourth."*—*"Seems like a few too many for such a short life—three great loves…"*— *"Why do they have to be great right away"*—his eyes laughed and she thawed out with a smile in return—*"maybe they were small and mousy—little tiny ones?"* Who the hell talks that way about their love, even if it's been trampled, even if it's all in the past, even if it's cut you in half like a truck severs a dog on the road, the way it did me that winter—the flight over the Atlantic: until five in the morning, right up until the taxi came to take me to the airport I *waited*—for a ring, if not of the doorbell (a thousand times, to exhaustion, my mind rewound the same clip: I open the door and you're standing in the doorway, barely containing with the corners of your mouth that insanely happy radiance that wants to leap from your face: finally, oh God, take your coat off already, how could you do this to me, you look a mess, so what happened, I've been going crazy here!) then at least of the telephone, a word, a voice, the end of a thread that I could catch hold of and keep unraveling from one continent to another, *I don't believe it!*—my insides screeched, scalded with grief, *I don't believe it!*—the taxi unloaded me into the snowdrift at the entrance to the international flights hall, how empty it was, how dead—a crematorium—the lights of Boryspil at five a.m., destination Devil's Dead End, the main gateway of the country, haha!—a country hopelessly *unconnected* to the nervous system that crisscrosses the planet, that thunders day and night, pumping through gigantic ganglions of ports, train terminals, and customs booths teeming streams of activated human neurons, Sheremetevo, JFK, Ben-Gurion, and wherever else I've been tossed about, even though all this is vanity of vanities, and vexation of spirit and body, but—there is motion, but—there is the animal pursuit of life, the wolf's bared teeth: another moment and I'll catch you, grab you by the scruff of the neck!—but in Boryspil, awakened by the desperately echoing click of my high heels, only unfocused, sleepy faces were rising from the luggage piled up along the walls, slowly unfurling their features like nocturnal animals roused from their sleep: as though they lived here, Jewish households in an eternal state of waiting until a crack opens in the border gate and they can scoot out, and so that's how my country saw me off, the country to which I, when all's said and done, will return—you betcha, despite the fact that my well-meaning American friends advise me to apply for yet another grant and assure me that my chances are good, I will return, come crawling back to die like a wounded dog, tied to the leash of a language that nobody knows, while you be sure to honor my memory in the *Review of Literary Journals*, that's right, and then there's my article from the year before last in the *Partisan Review*, which wasn't entirely stupid either, it was noticed, there was even a response in—wow!—the *Times Literary Supplement*; but the main point, my friends, you missed anyway, it seemed funny to you and no more: that the Ukrainian choice is a choice between *nonexistence* and an *existence that kills you*, and that all of our hapless literature is merely a cry of someone pinned down by a beam in a building after an earthquake—I'm here! I'm still alive!—but, unfortunately, the rescue teams are taking their time and on your own—how the hell are you supposed to get out? She felt herself alive for a moment in Frankfurt where they changed planes: when running blindly down the corridor she ran into two upright-standing border guards, two identically red-haired burly German guys with identical splotchy freckles all over their arms who, checking her out with a healthy youthful curiosity and exchanging good-natured growls in their own language, examined her passport and asked, just for the hell of it, in distilled international English where she was going—to Boston? Oh, it's very cold there right now, the coldest winter in a hundred years!—"I know," she said, giving a perfunctory smile like she was striking a soggy match, and, warmed by the animal, purely physical vitality steaming from them she suddenly felt, for the first time in her life, a literal uncontrollable urge to *wring her hands*: no longer a mere folk-song expression, no!—wring your hands, your white

hands, every finger, too; you'll not find, my dear girl, a
Cossack's love more true—but rather the most urgent,
insuppressible physical desire to wrest, with this desperate
gesture, her still living body from the tight armor of agony
that squeezed her from all sides: Mykola, Mykola, she wrote
him later from Cambridge, into thin air, to his local post
office for "general delivery" because there was no other
address—what are you doing, my love? Why are you turning to dust that which could be such an insanely brilliant—
life, passion, a flight of two forever-linked stars through
the fin-de-siècle night? Shit, now might be a good time to
reread that stuff—the style alone could inspire a fit of
hysterical laughter!—School of Medicine! that's where one
should take courses in Ukrainian romanticism, in the
psychiatry departments! *"You'll return my letters,"* she
instructed dryly as they parted, not that she had any great
desire to own those letters, what's over is over, hell with
it—but to free from his possession any vestiges of herself
that contained even weak signs of life, that still stung and
very much so; he turned the lock instantly, raising high his
dangerously well-endowed chin (no contest from all the
super-sexed Hollywood spermatosauruses): *"I wouldn't think
of it. They're mine"*—the only thing that's yours, sweetheart,
is what you've painted, and there's no point fooling yourself:
what you can't get into totally, blindly, over your head, will
never become yours. Write down those words, I'm giving
you permission, why not. And one more thing, almost
forgot: that's why those loves of yours end up being so small
and mousy—the little tiny ones.

"*Listen*," she was saying toward the end, timidly extending her voice toward him, like her hand under the covers during those oppressive silences at night when he lay beside her wide-awake, hoping she wouldn't notice—"*maybe you just simply never loved me?*" Because then everything really would be simpler: easier. But he would turn his face, cracked with a bitter smile, toward her—my God, what painful, unrelenting thirst this profile used to induce in her: like staring through a thick glass pane at a glass of ice water coated with condensation after not having a drop to drink all day; and now that glass pane was all that remained—he looked at her with the eyes of a sick animal: "*You're starting that again?*" Forgive me. I know you loved me—you loved me as best you knew: inside yourself, not outside yourself, I got the crumbs under the table, just like that little mouse—just a glance radiant with excitement, which sometimes broke out into a brief, reserved hug, an almost shy, crudely boyish poking somewhere at the side of the neck: "*You're a cool chick!*" and still yet eruptions of unfeigned joy at the sight of me, even when I'd pop in off the street and catch him at his canvas, and this was the same as throwing a bucket of cold water at a person fast asleep: he'd jump up wildly from the canvas like a startled colt, with a neigh of terror, instantly winding himself into a defensive pose, fist ready to plow you in the mouth—and a second later—ah, it's you!—his twisted face would change, shine, becoming the way it was that night, and also the way it would be when he removed my Post-it notes from his still unshattered windshield, because I bestowed them feverishly, with the speed of chattering teeth, I scattered them everywhere, eagerly polluting his entire space, little yellow butterfly squares, long fluttering handwriting like loose hair in the wind: hold on to me, hold on to me tighter, don't let me fly up to the sky!—and he did hold on, and he did carry around in the pockets of his winter jacket packages of notes resembling autumn leaves, some of which, the more important ones, he would paste into my books (my first autograph was from my first visit to his studio: I signed as though already predicting the inevitable collision of two avalanches: "sincerely conquered"—and right after came the first poems "from him," because my poems— I repeat, in case anyone failed to note it down the first time—were always *from someone*, even if that someone hadn't the faintest idea about it:

> More than a brother, you're homeland and home.
> (Hungry arms, hungry lips.)
> Neither of us died young
> Only to meet today:

"*You know,*" she blathered so very naively one night—"*I think we shouldn't get married after all!*"—"*Why?*"—he froze in the middle of the kitchen as though struck by an electric current, the Turkish coffee pot he was carrying toward the stove still in his hand: my poor darling boy, scared to death! "*Let's be blood brothers instead*"—she reveled with her whole heart at his fright while he noisily exhaled: it was a joke, of course, it was a joke!—by the way, we became brother and sister long ago, long before we met, because it was in search of you, my love, clearly in search of you that these incomprehensibly opaque lines of poetry rushed out of me, barely catching their breath, through all the years of my chaotic youth—I never allowed them to be published!—lines in which a "sorcerer-brother" peeked out here and there unexpectedly, lifted to the surface by some submerged force, a brother I'd never had: what I did have were friends, lovers galore, a wonderfully high-bouncing trampoline [albeit with holes all over the place] of social excitement: cool chick, you bet!—I had a husband, who taught me to accept and respect real love—my gratitude most profound, no joking!—the kind of love that grows with years and becomes the equal of life—but underneath all that churned a deep, persistent reverberation in the blood, threatening to materialize:

My sorcerer-brother
Where art thou now?
They will judge us without compassion
"Such are the times":
Not the ones in black cassocks
Not the headsman with reddish blade—
But the ones who come after us
Once the smoke clears.
Blades of grass will poke up
Through our dead, gaping mouths,
In my dead, charred bones
Demons will play sitting 'round,
And the place of my execution
They'll enclose with a sheer steep fence.
What kind of posthumous judgment
Awaits us, my brother, then?

Interesting question, no? There you have it. "More than a brother," turns out to be that same "sorcerer-brother": should have recognized him straight away, but why beat about the bush, I did recognize him—the minute I saw that series of witches' drawings: green-faced, should have been moonlit, but actually in the middle of the day, because the background is ochre, because the background is gold, a ritual song in a circle, but actually a wild dance, a "rite of spring," spreading smoothly from canvas to canvas—women with flowing hair in full-length white linen robes, arms waving, the dry crackle of hair [my own hair would also give off sparks when I brushed it hard!]—what are they doing, plowing a circle around the village to avert the plague? No, something darker, riskier, the goal is unclear—menstrual blood gurgles, trickling into the large bowl, a cock violently flapping its wings, no, *that far* I myself have never ventured: perhaps walked up close to it, but always backed away quickly, fearing insanity because there'd be an occasional howl or owl's cry in the dark, but this guy was digging the same grounds as I was, and the only one I'd ever known to do it, ah, shit—I sucked the saliva back through my teeth with excitement!—*better* than me: deeper, more powerfully, and damn, just plain *fearlessly*: full steam ahead, lungs full to capacity in rhythmic breathing—canvas after canvas, systole-diastole—he simply floated along in the stream that I could access only occasionally—only as a breakthrough, grabbing and carrying off a single poem in my teeth, my God, how truly wonderful it is to see someone *stronger* than you!—"So, Mykola, so what does all of this mean?" whined an "art expert" who, like yourself, had come up here from Kyiv, moistly sliding over her badly pronounced Ukrainian sibilants, though not slipping into Russian "out of respect for the guest of honor" and occasionally pulling strands of hair back behind her ear with trained, truly beautiful fingers—not a single art event could get by without these piranhas especially when horny bohemian artists were involved, or so you muttered to yourself, all irritated, because you were already drawn in, because you already desired his undivided attention, but then you couldn't run up to him squealing like this little fool—"Is this some kind of folk uhm...ritual? A supersition?" He gave a reserved nod—and thus seemed to be entering a secret pact with you; "What kind of ritual?"—"You can't talk about it," he replied solemnly: yes, brother, precisely, you can't, it's our secret, yours and mine—a seal on our lips like a dry kiss: turn the lock, hide the key, silence).

"*You see*"—in one of their first weeks of living together—new country, new continent, now everything was sure to be different, turning over a new leaf, yeah right—he was showing her perhaps the first of his new sketches, one not from the "reserve," an ink drawing—"*take a look, baby, this—is love.*" Love looked like this: "baby," a rather abstract naked woman, was lying in bed ("*You slut, dumping your tits out for all to see!*"—but that came later...) and playing a violin ("*What's this*"—she exhaled a sardonic laugh: sex was painful again last night, not that he noticed—"*a metaphor for masturbation?*"—"*Could be*"—a carefree nod of agreement, her reproach passing over his head: far too focused on the sketch to notice—"*it's from a Polish ditty I once heard and happened to remember*"); the woman's bottom half was modestly hidden by a sprawled-out, richly textured cat. Well, no mystery there, he was the cat. (*"Aha!—now you're caught!"*—his eyes glistened almost gleefully when he heard that according to the Chinese horoscope she was a Mouse:—*"Because I'm—the Cat!"*—Hmm, she didn't particularly get along with cats, and in general she preferred dogs, never missing a chance to pat even the mangy stray on the head, but at that moment—at that moment she was overcome by a strange, paralyzing ache of the already-present danger, it was both sad and sweet: yes, she was caught, and there was no getting away, game over—it's just that as she looked at the sketch she thought, with an internal shudder: what if that cat were to arch his back and sink his claws in *there?*...); at the foot of the bed stood a leafy potted plant of some sort, and on top sat a bird with a wedding band in its beak (*"Hey, when I get there—we'll get hitched!"*—he had hollered happily and offensively into the phone when she was finally able to get through to him—after that awful Cambridge winter, when her love slowly froze out of her, freezing into those impenetrable snowbanks, flowing out of her like bodily fluid from a skillfully punctured torso until it gathered in only one fiery point: just let him be alive!— and when she managed to find, finally, through networks of common acquaintances, some kind of phone number, and heard that familiar voice, which cooed in shameless satisfaction: *"So delighted to hear from you, my lady"*—she exploded like a Fury, barely containing every expletive she could think of—and he, as it turned out, had had yet another accident, right before she left, fell down the stairs at night and landed on a pile of rubble, broke his ribs, is still walking around in a brace, oh no!—she covered her mouth with her palms remembering in a flash a physiologically revolting dream she had had: like she was holding a sculptured bust of him in her hands, so frightening in the way it moved its lips, what the hell was that about, really! Okay, okay, I'll make it up to you, fella, you'll get a trip to America, a stipend, an exhibit in New York, wine-women-song, you'll have it all—only that "get hitched" lashed her like a rough screech, a solo part on a handsaw in the middle of an opera overture: wrong, wrong—the words all wrong!). Violin, cat, potted plant, bird, wedding band—*"they're in love,"* and the sketch did emit, it seemed to her, some kind of feeble warmth (in its final form, on canvas, painted after the breakup, this warmth had dissipated completely—the woman in bed ended up in the middle of a bilious-yellow desert, and after the painting spent the night in the basement belonging to poor Mark, totally discombobulated from dealing with psychotic Ukrainian geniuses, they found on it a dead spider—the best thing to do would have been to attach it to the painting permanently, somewhere between the kitty and the birdie, it was the only thing missing!). Several weeks later, however, a new sketch appeared—same woman, facing in the diametrically opposite direction, stretched out on a gigantic bone that had been gnawed white: *"That was her last man,"* he commented balefully—*"she ate him."* The background came out black, the bone glimmered against it with a sickly phosphoric paleness, and the woman's hair—standing on end as if raised by an invisible vacuum cleaner—was a fire-engine red. A diptych of sorts. A history of a love affair, if you will. *"This our love affair,"* she once blurted casually, still back home; and he, without shifting his eyes steadfastly fixed on something straight ahead, shook his head firmly: *"This is not a love affair. This is something else."*

Ladies and gentlemen, I can see the bored expressions that have settled onto your faces; in your minds you've already established the diagnosis: "severe psychological problems" on both sides—a nationalist-masochist (although this particular disease you're probably unfamiliar with...) and an autistic maniac (this one is simpler because in addition to purely communication issues, that inability to connect or whatever you call it, one might mention a few milder though clinically more significant symptoms—for example, the impossibility of keeping a phone number in his head long enough to write it down, and the especially characteristic, strangely awkward calligraphy—unexpectedly skipped letters, or a sudden capital in the middle of a sentence, or those illiterate "Ј" or "Э" that somehow wandered in from foreign alphabets, supposedly in order to make the written line more balanced graphically—bad things, troubling, and then if you were to recall those suspicious migraines of his that he boasted of fainting from occasionally, the case begins to look very serious)—no denying it, that nice, handy word *problems*; it can mean a math question, and breast cancer, and loss of love, and in every case there is always someone who can help: a professor, a doctor, a psychoanalyst—assuming, of course, that you have something to pay them with, and if you don't, then you'll just have to try and get it, go digging through all your socks and mattresses, nothing to be done—life is expensive: like Rosie, for example, Mark's wife, going to see a psychoanalyst for

seven years straight, two sessions a week, which poor Mark
(an oversized schoolboy), not yet even a full professor, is
obviously unable to pay for, therefore every once in a while
Rosie, the forty-year-old girl, the mother of a grown child
but tiny and thin as a sparrow (tight-assed sparrow with
thick werewolf browns meeting on the bridge of her nose),
invariably ill either from a chill or too much sun or at the
very least from exhaustion (hand on forehead like a collective farm worker, a crumpled wad of Kleenex by her nose),
must go looking for a job, and she finds something for a
month, or two, or even three—and all so that she could
go lie down on that couch twice a week and tell someone
who's willing to listen to her how unhappy she is—after
six years of this she and Mark stopped having sex and
this is obviously progress: now they're both gritting their
teeth on account of this abstinence, fights break out with
a hungry crackle, like a fire on well-dried twigs, at each
verbal interaction, and it seems that the number of therapy
sessions will have to increase: "problems" are "problems"
and society ordains that we solve them with four arithmetic
operations: there's A, there's B, you can add them, multiply
them, divide, or transpose them, and all that in the hope
of getting a third quantity, a full-time occupation!—somewhere in the back of the workbook lie the answers in fine
print, let's be patient, someday they may show them to us.
Someday each of us will read his or her answer—except
that by that time it will be too late to change it.

Ladies and gentlemen, problems—are things to be
solved according to a set of rules. But it's precisely those
rules that we don't know, we know only the four arithmetic
operations, and we push ahead with them, pretentious

ignoramuses, up to precipices and subterraneous caverns of unknown and imagined quantities, and the ground slips out from under our feet, and an echo resounds as through the canyon, and in that rumble you can catch a peal of— laughter (guess whose, come on now?), and a scorching horror takes possession as you suspend your foot over the void from which rise invisible fumes from a slow burn of that devastating sorrow that the Russians define as *deathly*, which sucks everything out of you till your bones ache: and so here we have—the doors to hell, ladies and gentlemen, welcome, they're always open, why are you dallying, isn't *this* the place you've been in such a rush to get to?...

"I've always wanted only one thing—to reach my full potential." That's what he would repeat, and he spoke the honest truth. *"Smell it, come over and smell this—aah, what a smell!"*—he would lean over a set of newly acquired paints, lustfully flaring his nostrils, ecstatically shutting his eyes (these American stores are sheer heaven, they've got everything, the bastards, look, look!—he surreptitiously stroked a silky sheet of Chinese drawing paper with his fingertip, what does it cost? are they nuts!?—and see this sponge over here, feel it, it's alive!—and they sell canvases already stretched, this is bloody unbeliev- able, and what are these? whitewashes? how much? they can fuck themselves, assholes—come on, let's get out of here— then an abrupt halt, twisting his head back, breathing in the air with the pain of unquenchable passion: can you smell it?)—she enjoyed this animal sensuality even if not directed at her, even if all she got were the crumbs: her love of words was equally sensual—first the sound, but the sound pulled

in with it, in its tightly woven trammel, a catch of texture, consistency, smell, and obviously color, too: color imbued not only individual words, it was especially pronounced when switching from one language to another—each, of course, radiated its own, brilliantly shimmering *basic tone*: Italian—electric violet, ultramarine, the kind of light effect you'd get if you could turn red wine blue; Polish shushed and grated fresh young bitter-tart garden greens; English slowly bubbled something translucent akin to a gentle golden chicken bouillon broth, incidentally a lot more watery in the States, the British variant more intense, thick-and-gooey, richer; obviously her mother tongue was the most nutritious, most healing to the senses: velvety marigold, or no, cherry (juice on lips)? strawberry blond (smell of hair)?...it's always like that, the minute you peer more closely the whole thing disintegrates into tiny pieces and there's no putting it back together; she hungered for her language terribly, physically, like a thirsty man for water, just to hear it—living and full-bodied with that ringing intonation like a babbling brook at a distance, just a lap—honestly, she'd feel better!—at that moment he remembered, unsmiling, how once, in about fifth grade, he was sitting in a Ukrainian-language class and secretly sniffing some paints hidden in his desk, and the teacher ran over and flung them clattering in all directions down the aisle—well sure, only a Ukrainian-language teacher would pull such a stunt, for some reason they seem everywhere to be the dumbest, most vicious hags (as if specially selected), rabidly faithful lackeys, abundantly loyal sergeants in the Soviet army—*you don't suppose there's a national inferiority complex rampant there?*...So they chatted—when they were still talking to each other, because he opened up to share something inside him only very gradually, creakily: he wasn't used to it, whatever little internal doors he had in there must have been wedged shut a ve-e-ry long time ago, and the hinges rusted out—God, what kind of a marriage did this guy have, I wonder, huh?...For outsiders, and that means everybody except one or two close friends (they had hundreds of common friends, but she realized fairly quickly that not a single one of that crowd, even the fairly smart guys he'd been friends with for umpteen years, really knew him all that well; he knew them—*saw* them!—in a much deeper, more penetrating, and at the same time somewhat more *ruthless* way, when they discussed common friends—which is, after all, utterly essential for every couple, because that's how the newly constructed *world of both* is populated, settled, in their case given to them pretty much ready-made, on the Biblical "seventh day"—she was struck unpleasantly by how coldly he dispensed judgments in all directions: X "sees things superficially," Y is an "extinct volcano," Z "married that huge babe 'cause he needs a mama"—like driving ash stakes through their hearts: nailing them down, hammering from the shoulder, without a hint of empathy, never actually touching upon their lives with his own feelings, and when ultimately he turned that side of him against her, calmly cutting off one of her "how am I supposed go on living?" questions with a harsh: "*I see in you an ability to survive under any circumstances*"—she immediately rose up to demonstrate this ability: absorbing not the painfully distant tone but rather the naked essence of what was said: the guy's tough, and smart, and he's been around, if that's what he says then maybe it's true, I'll survive?)—so then, for outsiders he smeared himself with a thick coat of an

impenetrable, though, one must admit, very masterful sort
of chitchat, all kinds of gags and games generously flavored
with spicy irony, but she was not one to be fooled by that,
she also had her (hah!) elaborate and ever-so-tightly fitted
(not to say sexy) linguistic mask, and when he tried to hide
behind his—hey, there, if you're gonna play, no cheating!—
she preferred to slice that papier-mâché apart with a knife:
and that's when the hysterics began, night after night, the
blade grew notched and dented, practically ended up in a
hospital, but she did the guy in, too—God help her: if this is
the way it's gonna be, then fine, I'm not the only one going
down! Fuck, how disgusting…"*You know what your precious
'hermeticism' is?*"—because he had named it thus, giving this
business a theoretical foundation, fucking deep thinker, a
conceptualist!—"*Well what? Go ahead, but keep it short, in two
words or less.*"—"*No problem, I can do it in two: a stone egg.*"—
"*Nice,*" he pulled in his shoulders for a moment, she got
him—"*but…well painted, right?*"

Try to wriggle out, willow-woman. Catch the air.
Sink your roots deep through the sand, to the
    moist virgin earth.
GULAG—is when they drive an empty half-liter
    bottle
Between your legs—after which they address you
    as "ma'am."
We are all from the camps. That heritage will be
    with us for a hundred years.
We search for love and find spasmodic cramps.
GULAG—is when you cry out, "My God, my God,
    why have you forsaken me?"

And there's no-one who gets what that language
is that you're shouting...

Thus she mumbles to herself (it's just that—is it *kórchi* or
korchí? the language is failing, failing, and don't try to fool
us with that "literature-in-exile" stuff!)—as she drags her
disobedient, unloved body up and down the streets of an
unfamiliar American city in which she has no friends, not
a soul, and at the department she has to smile and answer
each "How are you doing?" with "Fine"—yet another of
those arithmetical rules, even though what kind of "fayn"
can one possibly speak of, where the hell is it, who's seen
it around, that "fayn"—at one of the faculty parties the
graceful and composed plump Chris, an administrative
genius, mother of an eight-year-old girl, and of her husband, the eternal student (they survive on potatoes for
weeks at a time, it's a good thing they've been on sale at
Giant Eagle lately, ninety-nine cents for a four-pound bag)
confesses—flushed pink after downing the third glass of
free wine in one gulp and lighting a cigarette (ready to
talk her heart out)—that she's got breast cancer and has
been going for radiation therapy for five years now, and
she's only turned forty-one; while Ellen, always quick and
agile, electrically charged with excited laughter whether in
shorts, in a light summer dress with a shoulder strap sliding
down her arm, or in a tight black skirt with a side-slit up
to the hip, and a fluffy cloud of sparking deep-gold hair
bouncing with every step—she's almost fifty, divorced and
childless, spasmodically clinging to the "one size fits all
(ages)" image of a "sexy lady," from which the march of time
is relentlessly dislodging her, pushing her out the door no

matter how much she drowns herself in work in order not to notice it—constantly waving her cigarette like a priest his censer, exuberant, shouting how much she loves, just loves her visits to the gynecologist—has an orgasm right in the stirrups, and her listeners laugh along, an echo of her enthusiasm, fantastic, she's great, Ellen, the cool chick as that man would say—except that perhaps she gives just a li-ittle too much detail about herself: about how she was running late for class but the car wouldn't start, and how she had to run out into the street and hitch a ride, no-no, she didn't even need to raise her skirt, and how pleasant the businessman behind the wheel turned out to be, and what she told him, and how they exchanged business cards—all that schlock that one normally dumps on one's family every evening, because *that's* the place where we, girls, recount, to the lovingly sensitive faces turned toward us, everything that happened to us that day, but with out-siders—with outsiders you really need *skill* to dump this shit and not bore them, you must package it up like candy, in the crinkly gold wrapper of a humorous novelette, to rustle it enticingly—and voilà, they've swallowed it, and for all appearances you've entertained the crowd—Ellen falls a little short here, because in this you do have to be a bit of an artist or, as some would say, artiste, but aside from that—aside from that she is in perfect form, boisterously dancing on the open platform of the train that rushes her down the tracks to the outer limit of that day on which she finally—flags, sags, stoops, flame extinguished, as though someone has unscrewed all those unnecessary bulbs, and, perhaps, will also begin to frequent the psychoanalyst, just like sixty-year-old Cathy from the department down the

hall, whose husband left her a year ago and now it's impossible to get her to retire, or perhaps she'll secretly start drinking heavily at home, or get into meditation, or maybe get a dog—a purebred, it goes without saying. And then there's also Alex, an aging Serbian poet who's been roaming the world, shuffling from one university department to another, who claims with a dignified air: "I'm Yugoslavian," as if in this way he, like God, can wipe away the war and everything that came with it, his typical way of starting a conversation—"When I was in Japan…" "When I spoke at a conference at the Prado and the cardinal was invited too…" "When I lived in London, just outside the city, they gave me a whole villa…"—you could burst out laughing at how much this resembles the reportages, in the good old Soviet days, of those rare few "friendship society" types occasionally graced with a trip abroad appearing before a depressed and green-with-envy audience, each member painfully aware that they themselves wouldn't get "out there" in a million years; however, Alex has no such powers of self-reflection, nor powers to see or hear anything around him for that matter, being consumed as he is by the recitation of an enthusiastic panegyric to himself—to his books that have been translated into English, Spanish, Chinese, Alpha-Centauric; to his interviews and publications in such-and-such editions in such-and-such years; to how much he is paid by the page by *Word* and how much the *New Yorker* promises to pay—this monologue inside him seems not to cease for a second and occasionally reaches the point where it requires a set of ears—then Alex calls, stops to pick her up in his "Toyota" (each time inevitably mentioning that back home, in Belgrade, he used to have a "Mercedes"), and they go somewhere for a "dreenk," two Slavic poets in a foreign land, oh yeah, and this land can be covered with wheat, rye, and gold, inviolable coast to coast, Atlantic to Pacific, there's no way she's going to sleep with him and besides, he's far too much excited by his own oral biography to put the effort into pursuing her, but his poetry, which he's hauled over by the armload including the translations into Chinese, is really not bad at all—although mainly of the "snapshot" variety, travel sketches, a tourist's breakfast; still, in practically every poem a line peeks out that's truly authentic, and before you know it the entire poem has closed in around it: occasionally even, sparks fly from something truly wonderful, one night she asks Alex how he handles the language problem, for years hearing Serbian only from his wife, does he not feel the language resources diminishing—and for the first time a somber, wolfish expression visits his face: it's a problem, he admits as though forced to confess to a meticulously concealed physical defect—that's actually why he agreed to work for an émigré newspaper—aha, that would be the same as if she were to take in a job correcting the language of the New York Ukrainian paper *Svoboda* (ON THE DATE OF 31 AUGUST 1994 RESPONDING TO THE APPEAL OF THE ALMIGHTY CREATOR OF HEAVEN AND EARTH SHE LEFT FOR THE UNIVERSE (the Universe! in response to an appeal! is she a cosmonaut, or, pardon me, an astronaut?), LEAVING BEHIND UNSPEAKABLE SADNESS AND SORROW (in other words, she took off *without* sadness and sorrow?) OUR DEAREST, UNFORGETTABLE, FAVORITE WIFE, AUNT, COUSIN, AND SISTER-IN-LAW (whoa, let me catch my breath!). NOT HAVING THE POWER TO THANK EVERYONE PERSONALLY FOR SO NUMEROUS EXPRESSIONS OF SYMPATHY: TELEPHONIC, WRITTEN, AND

PERSONAL (hey, syntax! syntax, oops, sorry, *syntaxa*!) THAT'S WHY BY THIS PATH (how about trail? back alley? highway?) I EXPRESS TO ALL ACQUAINTANCES AND FRIENDS, AND FAMILY MY SINCEREST THANKS (okay now, try rewriting this thing so it makes some sense!)—and then she understands that this high from his own importance, this puppy excitement at every sign of his presence in the world—this is just one more way of creating in it a home for yourself, especially when there's no mutual interaction with either your language or your country, and also that it must take some time to reach this condition—and it comes as no surprise to her that after that evening Alex stops calling—probably forever. Oh Lordy, all of it, everything, requires skill—to be ill, to be lonely, to be homeless: each of these things is an art, each requires talent and effort. "Fayn"—we'll just have to learn.

He couldn't care less about her poetry, just like he couldn't care less about anything anywhere and always; he was led by the instinct of his own personal gift, and it was distracted by nothing. Knowing, with that dark, viscid knowledge— tribal and familial, which she carried within her since childhood like a swallowed rock and which, truthfully, drove her forward, forward, forward! by the insane fear of herself, too, falling into the ranks of the ordinary, *not making it*, going to the dogs like everyone in the previous generation, and the one before that, and the generation before that (those guys really went through hell—better not to think of it!), she spent her whole youth trying to break out of the vault filled with the poisonous stink of half-decayed talents, motionless lives rotting out, mildew and mold, the unwashed stench of futile endeavors: Ukrainian history—knowing, with that bloodline knowledge *what kind* of trapdoors that instinct of gift of his must have had to burst through, ramming them like a tank, in order to carry him out and up (always—up: his last works were also his strongest, they blazed with a light that was already otherworldly, like a starry sky over the desert— whereas in her own memory there was only row after row of "those who showed promise" who'd be raucously anointed to genius status and then roll en masse into the trodden ditch as soon as they had exhausted the vigor of youth!)—she, who would be overcome by nausea at the sight of the miserable native alkies in the mildewed remnants of their genius (if anybody's interested, check out the following addresses: "Aeneus" in Kyiv, and "Red Guelder Rose" in Lviv, free admission, feeding, and especially giving drink to the animals is not only not forbidden, but encouraged)—immediately demonstrated with him (the first one in her life!) the capacity to take a back seat: it was the first time that she was dealing with a male *winner*. A Ukrainian man—and a winner: a bloody miracle, can you believe it? In her wildest dreams she would not have imagined such a thing—the seventies and eighties alone in a provincial town (a.k.a. in the underground) would have been enough to do you in, that same town that her parents had to flee, holding her, a seven-year-old, firmly under her arms as they slipped through the KGB blockade; her father, who had served his six (Stalin's) years in the camps, was pursued, in the grip of terror, like a squirrel for the rest of his life by the specter of "recidivism"—nobody could handle a second arrest, even if they survived it they came out broken, each in his own way—I wonder if it wasn't those same "inspector-boys" in rustling coats, quick, all with the same standard-issue haircuts, all dark-haired, whose backs her poorly focused, blurred child's memory photographed as they rummaged through piles of books thrown over the floor surrounded by the all-of-a-sudden bare white walls of her first, no, her only home in her whole life—who later, having earned more stars and stripes, planted their deadly grip around the throat of the rebellious artist?—yes, my dear brother, and this damned blood-brotherhood of ours, like cellmates from the same concentration camp, shit, how many years, really, will that heritage be with us, and how the hell do we get rid of it, bleed it out? cough it out?—how?—my Kyiv friends, all mellow after a few drinks, reminisced on how they met him in 1982: they came out on some work-related trip, landed in one of the local coffee shops, and a baited-looking local approached them: "Guys, are you artists? I've got a studio nearby, come, I'll show you my work, I've got coffee too"—well, okay, as long as you're serving coffee, fine, pal, we'll have some—but what makes you think we're artists (they happened to be writers, actors, not exactly chopped liver, eh)?—"Uhm, but your beards"— hah! now that's something, so having a beard out in that rat hole was enough to put you on the watch list? Really? That's the way you squeeze your hand through the bars of a prison train-car window, casting a written note into the wind: maybe some good person will notice it and send it to the indicated address—peering out after the fluttering piece of paper, hungry hope in your eye: you're sure you're not artists?...And getting to the studio by back alleys, discreetly, circuitous routes: "It would be better if you weren't seen with me..." Homeland and home, yes: Ukraine, 1982. And no British correspondents, no letters of support from leading figures of literature and art—who was it that got the Nobel that year, Marquez, I think? (Damned good writer, and the fact that rumor had it that he was a good friend of the USSR, well—"who cares?") That story, which immediately made him so dear to her, so painfully felt from inside those hopeless years (which he overcame, won the match: by painting all that he painted!—while others drowned in drink, hung themselves, or, like her own father, stood smoking by the window for hours staring at the wall of the building across the way, getting lung cancer from the hopelessness of it all!)—that story she heard before the third day of the festival when he, under some lame pretext, managed to get himself to her hotel room, rudely awakening her from her sleep—everything, everything from the very beginning was based on chaos, on a violent break with established routine, on weakened senses, on wavering (like music on dying batteries) reflexes!—and he stood there, in an entryway as cramped as an elevator, his arms crossed on his chest, leaning against the door, his catlike eyes glowing at her expressively, and she was suddenly overwhelmed—she clenched her teeth so that they wouldn't chatter—by a flood of strange, you wouldn't say erotic, no!—a *different kind* of queasy, anxious arousal—like before surgery or a school exam: something thundered and thickened, moving in overtop of her, something bad, dark, and ominous, something autonomous and thus *real*, she might have still leaned out of the way, pulled her head down and let it pass by, but there was no fear in her, there was—an already switched-on, excited, and vibrant readiness to rush right out to meet life just as soon as it picks up speed, takes off from its well-worn habitual seat: something real is a rare opportunity, it's something that's bigger than you, something you must grow to attain, breaking out of your skin to get there, leaving it behind, seven skins, nine skins, just don't stop! Fine, I take up the challenge, look you in the eye! *"Until tonight then?"*—*"Until tonight."*— *"We'll go for coffee?"*—everything went up in turmoil, the whirlwind churned the leaves on the autumn roads and the town in which she was born and which had always been, somewhere at a distance like at the bottom of a lake, preserving her early, hidden, still sleeping childhood was now returning it to her—in an unbearably tender, misty light, this, actually, had begun on the first day already—the growing underground rumble of awakened memory, the recognizing of familiar streets: ah, so *that's* what they're like!—the display windows of the pharmacy on the corner, in the same place as twenty-five years ago—she stopped stock-still, choking on a surge of shining tears: this is where they put up the town Christmas tree, and she had her picture taken then with Santa Claus, a five-year-old girl in a bulky, furry coat, the smell of mandarins and lilac evening snow, its glitter under the streetlamps—and on the other side, a bit farther down, there was a theater, I think (matinee—holding Daddy's hand—a documentary of some kind, about monkeys?)—Oh, it's still there, even now, they told her with the forced benevolent smiles that one conjures to demonstrate sensitivity toward another person's childhood, and only he, whom she dragged with her by the arm—to that place: *"Shall we go to the park?"*—*"Wherever you wish, my lady, I am totally at your service"* (an old-fashioned park by the river, and again, the stone steps, as though freshly washed, emerge from the mist after many years, the peeling balustrade, ah, so *that's* where it comes from in my dreams!—and, oh dear God, this pulsating color, this languid, underwater lighting, cool bluish-green with walkways, trees, benches frozen in time, receding into the distance—my best poems, those most *mine*—are, therefore, also *from here*?)—*"There was a birch bridge somewhere around here back then"*—*"It's here now, too—let's go, I'll show you"*—only he alone did not pretend to be appropriately moved, he didn't pretend anything at all, he merely felt his way through her condition silently, focused and engrossed in his own thoughts, as he would do later at night feeling his way through to the cervix of her womb to exhale: hah, there it is!—they stood over the still pond covered in water plants the color of patina, *"Look,"* he nodded his head, *"what Zen"*—and suddenly painfully squeezed her shoulders: *"Listen, I love you and your bridge. Can you do that?"*—*"Do what?"*—*"Can you say—I love you and your Zen? You can't, because for you I'm just a person in the landscape: this landscape"*—now that would have been the time to ask: and what am I for you? Because she really did let him enter her landscape—every one of her landscapes, consistently, one after the other, ending up finally in Pennsylvania, while he, setting his course after her ("My final love," he boasted to his friends: they told her—while verses spurted from her like bubbles of air from the lungs of a drowning man:

Autumn. Early dusk.
Mire—and footsteps like rubber…

This love is not final,
You are wrong to think other)

—he passed through her territory like the Tatar hordes—
with wild whistle and howl scorching out from almost every
recess of her memory, from all of its main repositories,
that life-giving, secret, shimmering, loving *moisture* that
the soul gathers for itself year after year, for the dry years:
subterranean wellsprings, a constant and inaudible slurp
and suck, tenacious putting down of tiny, hairy roots into
the dark depths of the preconscious, into a corridor, which
suddenly opens—into the open space of a memory: a little girl stands swooning in the middle of an autumn park
walkway, feeling the drumbeat of the distant horizon for
the first time, feeling the world calling her, promising to
show her *the way*, everything begins with that little girl
and no matter what else happens to you in your life—it is
complete, it holds together for as long as you believe that
little girl, as long as you can access the call that she heard
way back then—because all those so-called youthful ide-
als—are nonsense, ladies and gentlemen, mesdames et
messieurs, "forget it," they are brought in from the outside,
that's why only the very few, and rarely, are able to remain
faithful to them, so hell with them, not a great loss, wipe
up your snot, all you bearded sixties lefties, ravaged and
crumpled by time, former hippies who never managed to
get it together for your own bungalow in suburbia with a
flower garden in the backyard and a two-car garage; and
also all you who did get it together, shaved your beards and,
unnoticed to yourselves, acquired a rich, glossy luster (like
glaze on a ceramic mug) of a life stopped dead in its tracks

in peace and prosperity; and all you Ukrainian rebels, once tossed into paddy wagons, pounded to pulp in cop stations and back alleys and now laureates of government prizes, your hands juicy and plump from too many state banquets and your so impressively broad backs corseted in Bloomingdale blazers—don't dream of your wonderfully turbulent youth even should some losers try to shove it in your faces, all that is nonsense, I tell you this sincerely—it's fallacy, delusion: truth is found only in childhood, only through it can we find the true measure of our lives, and if you have managed not to trample to death that little girl inside of you (or that little boy standing in the pasture with a stick in his hand, awestruck by the terrifying—because so beyond the human capacity to render—immensity of the multicolored symphony of fire of the setting sun)—then your life has not faltered, it has merely twisted and turned, no matter how difficult and painful the obstacles, in order to follow its own course, in other words, *it's been real*, and I offer you my congratulations—and love, ladies and gentlemen, true love—it can always see that hidden little boy (or little girl) in the other: "take me" always means: "take me together with my childhood" (*"Over here,"* she pointed, her dry voice faltering, as she leaned over in the passenger seat like a jockey on a racehorse—*"this is where you turn into the courtyard, this building here"*—it was the dead of night, three in the morning or so—he drove in under the arch, circled the car around, turned off the engine, *"Those windows right there, can you see, where the balcony is, on the third floor? That's where we lived"*—that's the moment he fell on top of her and with a long-repressed groan attached himself to her lips, his hands moving busily under her sweater, a little rapacious, but it was what it was, *"Let's go to your place...To the studio..."*—it's there still, somewhere, that courtyard, that balcony, that archway, and the old chestnut tree from thirty years ago still up on the hill—it's just that the girl who once walked out of that building into a fog wet and heavy with a mysterious hollow din—that girl is no longer there). Not true, you're still alive, she tries to persuade herself, massaging all the crevices of her memory the whole time, like a skilled surgeon with a body just pulled out of the rubble: what if I press here, can you feel that? what about here?—in fleeting glimpses, twitches of remaining reflexes, some things come forward from time to time—for example, yesterday when she walked out into the street came a painful recollection—a long, lightening-speed incision into the distant past—of the smell of autumn leaves, doesn't matter what you call these trees—sycamore, Canadian maple—the smell was the same as back home, moist, the aching bitter scent of *still-living* (living out its last days) vegetation: the sun in the high, thinning treetops, the beginning of the school year, the walk to school through a brilliantly gold-lit park, a small band of adolescents in billowing white T-shirts with strangely articulated quacking (English!) laughter rumbled past—their youthful eyelashes squinting against the sun, their mealy ripe wheat-colored bare necks and swinging arms disheveled by the brisk walk flashed by like behind a glass pane—a thought flashed through her head: none of you puppies have yet been struck by *real pain*—and who knows, maybe some of you will be lucky and it will pass you by?—and settled on this side of the glass, holding back the sobs pushing up against her throat: God, is it all really over—did it all come to pass, all that was promised at the dawn of life by that advancing rumbling call that had spilled into the universe; had it merely swept by—blowing in her hair, brushing against her lips, without reaching deep inside and extracting the most important?...(how fiercely he had roared: *I'll rip you to pieces!*"—scooping her up under the knees and planting her on top of him—and in the end not a single orgasm, unless this excruciating pain of being ripped apart alive is also a kind of orgasm?).

> At the end of the autumn road flesh wilts,
> And leaves rustle with the scratching of mice.
> The horizon becomes steadily more
> > bare—and The Lord
> Stands among the trees, clothed in white...
> So what now, Lord? What now?...

"Lord, which way now?"—that's what was written under a sketch that she spied in his workbook, which he carelessly left out on his desk: at the very tip, on a craggy peak of a mountain a shaven-headed man with dangerously defined facial features (like those of his author) balanced himself on one foot (all his faces were deliberately vague, all in some imperceptible way interchangeable and similar to each other, dispersing like ripples from an original that had been dropped into the water—the self-portrait that he never drew)—the man was holding a ladder pointed to the sky with both hands and asking God which way now, but the sky was empty. "*I've always wanted only one thing—to reach my full potential.*" Amazing coincidence, brother-dear, me too, but what exactly does it mean—to reach your full potential? Once upon a time—still beloved, still gleaming under her loving gaze like a freshly restored canvas: his eyes hard flashing emeralds, that unbearable (oh, I could scream!) profile from an old coin, that silvery, or rather glittery aluminum spiky hair (*"You little porcupine!"*—she laughed, stroking this dry, noble, sculptured head as she passionately pressed it between her breasts)—pure metal, stone, obsidian!—sitting in her kitchen, arms dangling between his knees, and staring motionlessly at the pattern on the floor tiles (that baggy sweater in which his tight, knotty body simply drowned she also fell in love with) he told her about his father—the old man was getting old out in a village somewhere in Podillia, let's go visit him together, will you come with me? (and right away she imagined him slamming the car door and proudly saying: "Dad, this is my woman!"—that colloquial "woman" instead of "wife" on the lips of Ukrainian men always jarred her but this time—this time she would not object, she would step out with a smile like from the cover of a woman's magazine in her gorgeous loose red Liz Claiborne coat and her black gathered boots with terribly high heels, right into the rainsodden black earth—or what do they have down there? clay? sands?—raising her collar, her manicured, thin, musical fingers with nail polish to match her coat, swinging her long silver Arabian-style dangling earrings: *his* proudly displayed trophy, total victory, with which a validated life renders an account before its progenitors)—his old man had spent his life in concentration camps, first German, then Soviet, *"lapped slops from the trough"*—he pronounced it like squeezing a pimple, with a certain predatory emphasis and sick pleasure at watching the puss-y core emerge—and finished his father's story quietly without ever raising his eyes: *"Slaves should not bear children."*—*"How can you say that, how dare you, it's a sin!"*—*"Because that stuff's inherited."*— *"The hell it is—what are you saying, that there's no freedom inside you?"*—*"Wanting to break out is not yet freedom."* **Break out!**—those words shook her to the core, so easily pulled from her own vocabulary, like he'd known for a long time which page to open first—with those words he *brought out into the open* and thus confirmed, authenticated the infallibility of her tribal instinct that had switched on that first night when she *recognized* him: my darling, my dear, dear boy, come to me, come into me, I will embrace you from all sides, hide you with my body, let you be born anew, yes, together from today to eternity, obviously we'll get married, never mind, we're already married, and we'll have a boy (*"You have to give birth,"* he'd said, catching his breath as he tore away from her lips like he could no longer bear to kiss standing up:—*"there's a lot of milk in you!"*—in his apparently nightmarish marriage—though he, mercifully, spared her the details, making do with a painful gesture—dropping his face in his hands as though washing it away: "It was hell..."—he *did* have a son, all grown by now, a student, and rumor had it a super great kid, in general he was the type to only produce *boys*, this she could establish instantly, with lightning-quick penetrating insight from when she was still a girl—with every man, whether she simply met him or slept with him: who would it be with this man, a boy or a girl, whose sex was stronger?)—a blond baby with fluffy chick-down hair had appeared in her sleep several times already, after spinning around in space it headed, launched by raging power of her passion—toward him:

he'll be a sturdy, wonderful boy, pure as gold (and their whole multifarious tumultuous past, the books they read, his paintings, her piano lessons, God, how much has been learned, how much contemplated!—swirled into the air in a colorful vortex, coalesced, and instantly created in her mind—*a nest*, became a structure—rounded and complete with a living gravitational center: not bad at all to be born into a world like that, and we—we'll be able to protect him, right? and anyway, how much of that Ukrainian intelligentsia is there among us anyway, pitiful, forcibly **dragged back** against the current of history—a tiny group and even that scattered: a dying species, almost-extinct clan, we should be breeding like crazy, and all the time, making love where and when we can, uniting in orgiastic insatiability into one, yelping and moaning mass of arms and legs, extending ourselves and populating this radioactive land anew!—our son, he, finally will be free of that legacy which we spent all of our youth settling accounts with—it's been so painful, we may have actually paid it off by now)—the fierce, sharp sexual instinct of *the breed*, once apprehended in its full breadth and magnitude, consumed and propelled her at random, clearing everything in its path—who cares about a smashed-up car, what are distances, whether between cities or continents!—no matter about a fire with summonses and police reports (what a strange fire that was, the investigation wasn't able to come up with anything, at a winter cottage where he had come up with a group of friends, he was lighting a fire in the fireplace in the wee hours of the morning, insisting on shish kebabs, he took off with his car, not yet smashed-up at that point, to the market, bought the meat—she remembered him carrying a heavy,

bulging plastic shopping bag in front of him striped with
rivulets of blood: the sleepless night had left her with a
cloudy, uneasy feeling—a dry, bitter taste in her mouth, a
strangely palpable sense of not having washed and having
dirt under her nails, at the time she thought it was because
of fatigue, too much booze and cigarettes; however, later,
in normal condition conditions [well, not normal, but what
you could call fantastic, with all the American consumer
conveniences] it became clear—nope, that wasn't the reason—the feeling was all the more odd because he was so
obsessively clean, spending an hour each morning in the
shower not counting the shave, she was even curious: what
can a healthy man be doing in there for so long, masturbat-
ing? she never was able to smell his real scent: cigarettes—
yes, deodorant—yes, but what does this man really smell
like, the one you've been sharing table and bed with for
two months, if you'll pardon the elevated style?—even his
sperm, it seems, had no smell, maybe because the second
he came he would jump up and tear for the bathroom like
a crazy man, hey, am I supposed to come with you, or what?

It was all—iniquity and dirt:
The washing of underground ores
From ancient resistant poisons,
After which there remained—a corpse.
Washed and without a scent,
Both arms thrown back,
Like the limb bones of wings,
He lay there, silent, and smoked.
I, too, remained awkwardly still,
As into me entered—hell

—that's what she writes now, what good-for-nothing shit—
the function of a sick organism, no more, but then—then,
through her insomnious stupor she could see the bluish,
starchy, light snow sparkle finely, frost glittered on the win-
dowpanes; it was quiet, a great, almost universal silence,
only leaves caught up in the fresh snow would rustle from
time to time underfoot, there were streaks of pale sunlight
across the hardwood floor when she walked into the hall
where he crouched before the hearth setting the fire,
edging the prepared logs to the center, he spoke up without turning his head: *"Can you hear that?"*—a capricious,
splashing sound carried down from the attic—*"the pipes
have burst, we'll have to call for a plumber"*—she gently passed
her hand over the back of his head, from the shoulders
up, against the grain as if expecting to set off some sparks,
what is she to do with this unease inside her, *"what am I to
do with you?"* when suddenly—she barely had time to step
out of the way—Lesyk flew into the room, coat askew, the
film zoomed in for a close-up—the lens twirled like a bal-
lerina: hysterically jubilant horror in his eyes, the mouth
gashed in a scream: "Everybody get out! Fire!"—who's on
fire, what's on fire, but they were already outside standing
dumbly, heads upturned: the whole mansard rumbled,
cloaked in a thick smoke underlit by a yellowish glow, it
was blustering up to the sky, and it was already guffawing
boisterously, *something* inside was building into a roar of
laughter, extending itself to full height, its head crashing
through the roof out to freedom, ho-ho-ho, at last!—and
again she for a split second was surprised that she felt no
fear, detached, as though none of this was happening to
her—a young woman was awkwardly running over from

the neighbors', for some reason wrapping a black kerchief around her head as she ran, someone ran off to make a phone call, faces and figures leaped about in the corner of her eye, commotion picked up all around, and yet all she saw was his strange, somehow otherworldly calm, his profile raised up to the low silvery sky, hands in pockets, she remembered the lines from a letter she received from him recently: *"I'm getting used to my present condition, but I need medicine. I'll accept hospital, prison, lobotomy"*—something was *not right*, and when after several hours, after the fire was put out, after all the screaming was finished, when the fire trucks were done with flashing their blue emergency lights over the snow but the police investigator had not yet arrived, and the group of friends, still in the throes of excited laughter, coughing, blowing of noses—the first shock was over, they had to unwind, didn't they—began polishing off the rescued bottle of cognac, the one that was to go with the shish kebabs, in the annex, which seemed all the more cozy after all that had transpired—they almost felt like family, well, folks, that was really something, wasn't it, pour me a little more, who wants some lemon, ah, heaven, that hit the spot, somebody get me a cigarette—and he suddenly went rummaging through the bag and pulled out a bunch of fireworks: bought them at the market that morning, he confessed, wanted to put on a little show—an explosion of nervous laughter shook the annex, even the panes rattled: well, well, well, you certainly did that—how did you pull it off? just don't think of showing those to the inspector, you hear?—he folded his wrinkles into a smile and turned to her, raising baggy eyelids with a quick dagger flash: *"Maybe now you'll have something to remember me by"*—earlier that morning, before the fire, she told him she was leaving for the States. The investigation found nothing, absolutely nothing—the fire had burst into the building out of nowhere, who? what let it in?—it burst in and proceeded to chase her for the next nine months, even all over the American expanses, in the kitchen, especially when she would come out to smoke late at night, she would pick up a distinct sulfuric scent every once in a while—was that gas leaking? skillets, with a cobra's hiss, would spit boiling oil at her legs, the burns healed slowly, and after he arrived they simply opened up like stigmata, God forgive me—he personally sealed up the blisters on her calves with a thin coat of ground eggshells: *"Sit still for a while until it dries"*—and she did sit still in front of the television set, humbly laying out on the "coffee table" her unevenly seared raw sausages, now completely devoid of any erotic charm—and finally, the last night before they were to, thank God, move out of that apartment which had been transformed during the time of their habitation into a furious box of thickly condensed, almost *visible* dark-brown cloud of torpor—where they were going it wasn't clear, into a motel for now, as long as there's some kind of a change—that time, as if to say good-bye, the fire returned in its original form: she was alone preparing dinner in the kitchen with the usual squeeze of anxiety growing into nausea as she waited for his return from the studio, scrubbing something with her back to the stove, and suddenly she turned around as if someone pushed her—the electric burner under her skillet was ablaze, fire almost up to the ceiling, and that same malicious laughter was coming alive within it, but this time she was facing it alone: the "fire alarm" was silent for some reason, like it was paralyzed, but she thought about that only later, in the first moments she automatically, without opening up her clenched fists—in the left one she later discovered some clutched onion peels—set to beating down the fire with the towel she had grabbed from somewhere—the hungry fire bounced with joy as though that's what it had been waiting for, the smoldering towel in her hand seemed to be melting like molten metal, curling swiftly, embers flickering along its blackened edges, until she remembered to start throwing water—one quart, another, a third—and it hissed, spreading in all directions with an acrid stench, she stood in the middle of the kitchen with the charred rag in her lowered hands: no, God, I can't take this, I can't take this anymore!—and so her prophetic dream came true—an old dream from a year ago, visited upon her long before they met: a sapling at the crossroads, trembling and rustling, someone invisible is setting a bonfire below, the strike of a match, and oh—in a flash!—the sapling is consumed by fire which goes out as soon as it starts, as if it only meant to strip its crown of leaves, and so in the place where a moment earlier the sapling glittered with shades of light green against the blue sky there now protrudes a bitter, blackened skeleton. On the occasion of which, girlfriend, allow me to congratulate you.

> A budding tree in a naked row—
> Why in such hurry, you foolish thing?
> The soaked earth, rusty and lifeless
> Still awaits its suede medley of green,
> The spring wind still hides like a mouse

Under branches lined upright like brooms—
And you're out here sighing, and
  you're out here trembling,
Sticky little leaves fluttering in the light!
Stretching up on your toes, poor child,
With all of your sap and nerves—
One can almost hear the languid crackle
Of your joints, still stiff from the winter...

—first came this poem, also unfinished—and couldn't you finish it, see it through to the end—was it that hard?—then the dream, then—everything that came after. So knock yourself out now, dig deep, layer after layer, you pitiful, pitiful archeologine—just don't you dare feel sorry for yourself, because nothing weakens you like self-pity). Who can tell us—poems, do they only predict or do they, God help us, construct our future for us—summoning from the teeming multitude of possibilities within it that one, which they *name?* And if this is really so—if we, blind maniacs, program our own lives in advance, pleased as punch at how cleverly we've written it all down!—and thus make our lives what they are, then this is a truly frightening gift, Lord, like a bomb in the hands of a five-year-old—and how does one pray to be released?

Who (what) writes through us?

Lord, I'm scared. I've never truly been scared before— not of external threats (those are nothing, there's always a way out), I'm afraid of myself. I'm afraid to trust my own gift. I no longer believe that it is—in *Your* hand.

Look down upon me. Please.

In the evenings she escapes to the library—mainly so that
she doesn't stay alone in the house, where despair waits for
her in the gathering twilight in order to throw a black sack
over her head—but the library can't save her: none of those
more or less well-written other lives, bound in folios with
worn spines, that stretch on and on, row after row, from
floor to ceiling on multi-storied shelving while she accrues
mileage walking up and down in search of the volume that
she's decided she must read—like in the universal cemetery
(gray sky, a limitless field out to the horizon of identical
gray headstones, and even though you know that behind
each there is a person hiding ready to hop out the minute
you call him, donning a perfectly living and full-bodied
shape, the mere astronomical quantity obliterates any
sense in choosing one of them: how many of them, after
all, will you be able to resurrect during the course of your
life, and how many of these resurrected and read entities
have meant anything for you? The most you can do—and
that is the maximum!—is to join their monotonous ranks
with yet another not particularly noteworthy slim volume,
and the "date due" slips glued on the inside covers indiffer-
ently demonstrate the absurdity of this whole enterprise:
according to them, in twenty years you turn out to be the
fifth person at Harvard to borrow *Briefing for a Descent into
Hell* by Doris Lessing—a novel that is mentioned in all literary handbooks and truly deserves it—and the *second* to
fancy the Polish edition of Milosz's work—whereas most of
those recounted lives simply gather dust, like uncollected
letters in the numbered pigeon holes of the "general delivery" window at the post office)—not one of those lives has
any relevance to hers, not one answers the question that

she cannot seem to avoid no matter which way she looks at it, no matter which direction her pathetic hopes turn in search of an excuse: *why not now? immediately? why wait?*

Beautiful children, we were to have beautiful children, an elite breed. Better not to recall that, right? Well, no, it doesn't seem to even hurt anymore: you remember—but with your thoughts, not your feelings (hard to say which is worse!). What's true is true, in slavery the nation degenerates—the crowds that fill Kyiv buses, all those stooped men with drawn, rumpled faces on bowed legs, the women buried under walrus-like gyration of raw-meat dough, young guys with retarded laughter and wolfish bite that bust in without regard to who's ahead of them (if you don't step aside—they'll knock you off your feet and not look back), and the babes with the crudely painted masks over their skin (remove the makeup—and all you'll find is a naked eggshell surface like in a De Chirico painting) and a persistent aura of some kind of clammy underbathedness—they're like objects made without love, any which way just to get it over with: had to meet the quota at the end of the quarter, or needed to produce a child to get on the housing list, or simply fucked somewhere in the alleyway or, after some heavy boozing, in a train corridor (she actually *rode* one of those trains once, from Kyiv to Warsaw, going to a poetry festival—just imagine!—a fierce horde of contrabandists heaving bags, a third-class sleeper car, six open berths per compartment, baggage piled up to the ceiling—*commodities*, that's how they called them, by their scientific name in reverence to our own Karly Marx—the stench of the toilet, the door from the sleeper car to the front corridor clung to one hinge, swinging open occasionally to the clatter beyond with a slow, slow creak, like the pain of grinding teeth, the accustomed yet still disgusted expression of the clean-shaven puppy mug of the Polish customs officer who collects—a bottle of vodka from each occupant of the *przedział*, and that's not bad at all, the matrons who have just shed a few years from joy rush to assure her as they smooth out their outer garments—phew! we got through!—and pull, from their seemingly bottomless sweatpants, two more miraculously spared bottles of hooch, each of which will go for ten bucks in Chełm: you should see what happened to us at the Yahodyn crossing once, where they told us—we'll take a woman for every bus, say yes and we've got a deal!—A-and what, did you do it?—Well, what else could we do?—at night she lay in the top berth listening to the cacophony of unevenly pitched snoring, painfully in love with her misfortunate people, and the people—they heard her and responded: a massive body loomed in the hushed darkness, a waft of heavy, aroused breathing against her face: "Mommy…baby… Cum'ere, you hear me? Hey, you hear me?"—getting more and more heated as he went—"Wat's wrong? Let's go pokey-pokey, huh?" an arm plunged under the blanket—"how about I play wit' your boobies, eh?"—she shot up, hollering in a well-rehearsed bass: "Back off, sir, please!"—the bitches on the neighboring berths played dead with fear—fear for their *commodities*, perhaps?—only a tiny granny by the doorway spoke up in a trembling voice: "Leave the girl alone, why are you bothering her?" "Mammashaa!"—he turned and growled—"Mind your own bizness!"—he did heave himself back, though, the mood had been spoiled: he had released some of his dangerously-building aggression, and that's when she started hollering loud enough to wake the whole train car; and he also, no longer lowering his tone or backing down, roared: "Dontcha worry, cunt, I'll find'ya and get'ya! I'll get'ya so bad, it'll be tits up for you in Chełm, you hear me?"—there was a stopover in Chełm and she ran, her coat under her arm, through all the train cars to the very back, the train conductor, a cachectic young woman with a blanched complexion shook her head with that old-lady Mother-dolorosa look—the things that go on in trains these days, God help us—and let her out the emergency exit—there was no step stool, she had to jump, first throwing down her bags—into the stinging moisture of the early-morning fog, straight into the gravel between the rails, drawing blood as she scraped her palm against it—and straight into the hands of furious Polish cop who'd been racing alongside the train like a greyhound—there's no exit here, ma'am, show me your documents—she practically threw herself on his chest, hugging him like a brother). Only much later, in fuzzy erotic fantasies (when she was getting divorced from her husband her hungry, lively, corporal imagination was released first—that's when that slippery-slope slide began—whereas her childlike, or rather, maidenly, barely twenty-year-old, staring-out-into-the-world-with-curiosity readiness for new love switched on only later, finalizing the separation)—returning in her mind back to that night in the third-class sleeper and picking it apart, she tried to play that unrecorded clip: how *might* have things played out, how and what is it that *those people* do—out in the

passageway between train cars, wheels clanging, back
pressed to the railing, groaning, convulsing together with
it? or maybe in the bathroom, astride the toilet seat with
ankle-deep runny mud smeared all around?—*what* do they
feel at that moment, what do their women feel—the sensual
luxury of humiliation, the perverse thrill of momentary
descent to the animal kingdom, or, perhaps, and this is far
worse, they feel nothing at all? but maybe, hell knows,
maybe this really is healthy sexuality in its purest form, no
complexes, no paralysis caused by civilization and all its
twisted perversions—only, damn it, why do they end up
having such ugly children, dwarfed, with faces of tiny
adults, expressions set, after about age three of four, like
cooled plastic in molds of obtuseness and spite? Once, and
not all that long ago, maybe only three or four generations,
ladies and gentlemen, allow me to assure you that we were
different, and the evidence can be clearly shown on the
screen—if we can find a screen and projector somewhere
in the auditorium—at least a few images—yellowed, pale
photographs of those times showing peasant families frozen in unnatural, stiff poses before the camera: father and
mother at the center with hands folded in their laps like
schoolchildren, no evidence of birth control whatsoever,
and above them towers a whole forest of personages—lads
like oaks, one sturdier than the next, a feast for the eyes,
uniform gazes sternly aimed at the lens from under their
heavy brows, their thick locks of hair painstakingly slicked
back, their ox-like necks bursting out of the tightly but-
toned collars of their dress shirts; the youngest, who seems
to be burning a hole in the photo with his fiery glance, is,
of course, still in his high-school uniform and cap, this

would have cost a calf every year: but God willing, he'll get an education, be somebody, because he was such a smart, quick little thing even as a tot—later they perished in all the national battles: Kruty, Brody, and wherever else, those who were to make up our elite—the girls usually posed in national dress: the jangling—you can hear it by just looking at it—heaviness of earrings, coral necklaces, braids and ribbons cast over shoulders, the shimmer of densely embroidered upper sleeves, the rough cut of their skirts and vests does not conceal the luxuriant healthy bodies, ready to give birth; I, however, would like to draw particular attention to the faces, ladies and gentlemen, these beautiful, expressive faces which must have drawn a fair deal of input not only from God's carvers but also from the many years of lives spent in toil, lives which—if only you don't insist on constantly ravaging them in search of their sense and meaning, as we fools so often do, and accept them as they are given, like good and bad weather—gradually smooth away from your face all the secondary layers, baring the lean purity of the original—could it be God's?—sculpture: everything superfluous is tucked in, cleaned up, the foreheads fill out, jaws become more determined, and—the eyes, eyes, eyes shine ever-deeper, the black earth has risen, as the poet wrote, and its glance from time's distance—is frightful and scrutinizing—what happened to all of them afterward, did they all really die out in the 1933 Famine? Did they perish in the camps, in the NKVD holding cells, or did they simply work themselves to extinction on the collective farms? Good God, we used to be a good-looking people, ladies and gentlemen, open faces, strong, of good stature, self-willed, and firmly rooted in the ground from which many have tried long and hard to rip us out with the flesh until they finally succeeded, and we have flown off, scattered over all the expanses liked plucked feathers from the guts of pillows ripped apart by bayonets, pillows lovingly harbored in hope chests in days of old—for we were always waiting for our big wedding, embroidering songs for ourselves, cross-stitched, word after word, and so throughout our entire little history—well here we are, embroidered. Slavery degenerates a nation, I tell you this yet again, I'm gnawing on this thought until it has no more taste, just so that it would stop gnawing me, like bad weather, like monthly pain in an empty womb— *survival*, as soon as it takes the place of *living*, turns into *degeneration*, that's right, my Jewish brothers, my dear Ashkenazi, in case any of you happen to be tucked away in this audience by chance—this glass is raised to you, too: you can cast your contemptuous guffaws at the Sabras— dullards, so to speak, hicks, or whatever you call them there—but I will never forget the envious, up-and-down gape of a Kyiv colleague who first saw them, he himself was a small-built, lively demisang with narrow, feminine, raised and tucked-in little shoulders which imperceptibly gave his side view the profile of a hunchback—we traipsed all over Jerusalem together, passing by the hundred-and-umpteenth patrol unit, and the poor guy—couldn't help himself, gave in: sixty years old, still from Brezhnev's time, a professor, and a boy who greedily glues himself to a hole in the fence to watch the military parade, a tiny hunched pillar, and as the patrol unit marched off a secret whisper called out something buried even deeper than all the Soviet demisang complexes: "God, they're gorgeous!"—and those soldiers truly were a sight, like they were deliberately selected—mythological Titans accidentally dressed in camouflage uniforms with automatic rifles over their shoulders, broad mountain-plateau shoulders, movable tree-trunk thighs, strong, bluish teeth glowing against olive tans, as though earth itself came to life and stood up to stride, ah what men, a joy to look at!—in Eastern Europe go try to find yourself such luxurious Semitic giants—it was as if there, among dry hills burnt to ochre, Biblical history proceeds uninterrupted; at any rate *these men*—in uniform and hoisting automatic rifles who combed the Arab and Christian quarters, moving in the sunlight with the lazy grace of sated predators—*could have* been the descendants of Abraham and Jacob, whereas my professor—if only because with those little shoulders, pulled in either from cold sensitivity or merely apologetically (cover up, hide, clear your throat obsequiously, and blend with the furniture), he subverted the veracity of the Old Testament: you can't wrestle angels with shoulders like that, you can't do much of anything at all except run the tightrope, which is what he did his whole life, as did millions of Ashkenazi, sinking deeper and deeper into their chest cavities with every generation, and then the tightrope snapped, like in that ditty, and everything came crashing down, oh my God, did it ever! Nonetheless, they do still have those hills, burnt to a yellow ochre, where history goes on, but where is *our* Jerusalem, can somebody please tell me, and where do we look for it?

Out there in Jerusalem, going from temple to temple, she
pleaded with God to give her strength—no more than
that: the year had turned out to be difficult, lonely (her
marriage, which had been decaying slowly for a while,
fogging up her soul like a window in a room full of heavy
breathing, finally fell apart), but mainly—homeless, full
of fitful jumps from one temporary shelter to another, just
so she wouldn't have to remain in the tiny flat with her
mother: staying with her had made her hate her own body,
its stubborn, insurmountable materiality—it had to, no
matter what you did, fill up a certain cubic measurement
of space—at nights she dreamed of herself as a man—a
tall, long-haired, swarthy male Mowgli who drags an old
witch with bluish-gray, disheveled hair into bed and *can't
have sex* with her!—American psychoanalysts would have a
ball with that one if someone were to let them know about
it!—and that's when it began to appear—in tiny flashes
and jerks, dashing out and running for cover again—a
feeling of all-out complete exposure to all forces: have you
come for good or for evil? In her mind she assured herself,
clenching her teeth: I don't care if it's worse, as long as it's
a change!—and her poems promised:

> Tonight, terror will probably come.
> Hot shivers—of lovemaking or vomiting—
> Foreboding debauched coupling
> Or death's cry—shake the ailing body.
> Rupture, rupture—all ligaments, nerves, veins:
> My defenselessness is now so total,
> Like an overt call to evil: Come!
> I've already seen myself as a building

In which an orange rectangle burns
  in the night, a bare window,
With planks across the chest
And bottom of the abdomen, like for an X-ray,
And the rock, the one to shatter the pane
Already lies there, waiting for the hand.

There you go—shit, what else can you say here…But in
Jerusalem there seemed to be a bit of relief, after all, the sym-
posium turned out to be kind of interesting, so she was able
to swallow fairly easily that bone of personal professional
exhibitionism forcibly inserted into her throat: each time
demonstrating yet again to grinning Western intellectuals
that, see, Ukrainians also speak sentences with subordinate
clauses; it's just that when she was sitting at a table on the
open terrace and blissfully stretching her legs during a
break between sessions, imbibing sips of coffee together with
conversation—they were arguing about Dontsov, please try
to understand, folks, that was not anti-Semitism—it was the
roar of a wounded beast: let us go, let us live!—and, with
a concealed smile, examining her interlocutors through
the golden slivers of her squinted lashes, she suddenly
heard a sharp, powerful yowl: from out of nowhere a huge
anthracite-black cat had appeared on the terrace and proceeded to walk among the tables, tail held high to general
laughter and multilingual exclamations, still ripping the
air with unrestrained shrieking—a cold shiver crept under
her skin: what the hell kind of apparition is this now?—but
the cat, bastard, kept heading straight toward their group
and, arching its back, jumped straight into her lap, curled
into a warm heavy ball and huddled quietly, twitching its

perked ears and switching into a deep purr: it found what it was looking for. Everyone had a good laugh then; with unconscious fear, she carefully petted the beast as if to appease it—the tom bared its hard, glassy eyeballs, golden with deep black slits for pupils, like from the bottoms of inverted candles; in her mind she gasped: oh-oh-oh!—you were caught, sweetness, that's when you were really caught— exactly half a year earlier, half a year before everything was swept up in a deafening whirl and carried you off, not giving you a chance to catch your bearings: and you thought of yourself as some kind of rescuer, a Myrrh-bearing Mary, yes? Well, you got it—right where you wanted it, smack into that yellow-lit rectangle with planks across the chest and abdomen, so don't go whining now—he did, when all's said and done, love you, that man. No, it was *something else* that wanted to love you through that man: a cat in your lap, a cat in your bosom, a flash of eyes and claws, while I, prostrate, am playing the fiddle and screaming: you're hurting me, my love, you're hurting me, do you hear me?

Explain one thing to me. Explain it, because I just don't seem to get it. Do you really think that if you have a hard-on and you don't come right away this makes you a prince and the woman must kick her legs in the air and squeal with delight every time you deign to touch her—in the middle of the night, after you've folded up your little pictures so very neatly and I'm in the grip of my first dream? Although, pretty soon after his arrival she stopped having dreams—or more precisely, she stopped remembering them: some kind of clumps of generally dull, brownish or asphalt-gray tones merged in a cloudy swirl, but not a single plotline emerged into daytime consciousness, like a huge lid had fallen down to divide it from the consciousness of the night—the simple awareness of his lying beside her shut down all channels of connection. Perhaps for the first time in her life she found herself imprisoned in the cage of naked reality—the world became opaque, the second bottom—the flickering, underwater net of secret meanings, which up until now had always shone through in her dreams and poems—switched off and extinguished itself with a click; there were now no more dreams and, consequently, no more poems either: she lost her bearings as though she had lost one of her senses, went deaf or blind. Her body, shattered by night, always felt heavy and awkward, somehow bloated inside, like she really was pregnant—a bag of meat from the market dripping blood, what's going on, she wondered dully, why am I always feeling so bad—and would fall asleep on his arm like she fainted, while he happily mumbled at her ear: "*Hmm, it seems that you're capable of being an even very 'delightful babe'—just that you've to get this sex thing straightened out.*"—"*Sex,*" she would murmur like a teacher, already half-asleep: her brain still being the last thing to switch off—"*is only a sign of deeper disagreements.*"—"*I doubt it,*" he'd cut her off and close the subject. So it seems like you don't know all that much about this business, my pet—notwithstanding all your extolled experience, who would have thought? *Talking about it*, to simply reach mutual understanding was impossible—he'd get angry right away, jump into a defensive posture; whereas stretching out her arms to him during the day would evoke in her a lighting-quick queasy feeling of losing balance—like in an elevator that comes to a sudden stop, or when you're rushing alone against the crowd that has just poured out at the trolley stop—it turned out he "didn't like to be pawed," indeed this aversion to intimate contact was plain unhealthy (*"Aren't you ashamed of pawing men this way?"* he would sneer, squinting one eye over the pillow)—by that time she was willing to wail, not just talk—in an endless 24/7 monologue (the way undigested food propels itself out of the digestive tract from both ends), to shake him by the shoulders, to shout loud enough for him to hear, what is with you, you jackass—and the jackass, incidentally, arrived with the intention of starting a family, no kidding, just picked up and showed up in whatever he was wearing at the time, that's love for you!—and kept reproaching her that while he's hanging out here with her, they're probably stealing bricks form his construction site back home, *"So you what,"* she would place her fists on her hips: a witch, a bitch from the prison zone, she had no idea she could be like this—*"you'd like me to pay you for the inconvenience?"*—ah shit, how is this possible that two not entirely stupid people, who supposedly love each other, right? who overcame so many obstacles in order to be together, what he had to go through to get the visa alone, after all the car crashes and broken ribs, what she went through that winter in Cambridge—that they should be incapable of reaching even an e-le-men-ta-ry understanding—it's mind-boggling! And—it was probably in such moments that his wife used to throw those knives at him, like against a brick wall, something he once admitted reluctantly—cute, a family sport of the Ukrainian intelligentsia, how about that: and so what happened? she was itching to ask, did she miss? Instead she tried to be rational: listen, I'm not a puppet on a string, am I now, why are you treating me this way—he'd snarl back, bent over the desk and glaring from under his brow, like he was releasing smoke rings of his rage: *"It's just that many things inside me have been killed!"* Thank you, dear, it seems that from now on I'll be able to say the same. In other words, it's contagious, this disease of the spirit? In other words, it's now better for me, too—to avoid people, better not to get close to anyone? You have taught my body to castrate the perpetrator: all of my feminine strength, accumulated for generations, which has thus far been directed toward the light (the most precious memory of previous loves is the sun against a dark sky: that's how it's seen in outer space, it's *from there* that my fragile little vessel has filled itself to the brim with streaming joy), with you has turned itself inside out, black lining outward, has become destructive—death-bearing, if we don't mince words about it and put it plainly.

> I'll kneel where I stand: oh, there's been
> A ter-rible, transgressive sin—
> To this day I quake, vomit thrusts at my throat,
> Grinding hummocks of frozen ice
> In my gut! In my chest!
> Whom can I beg: blow it out,
> This dry blue blaze
> Lift this weight off my chest?

Because, I am guilty after all, because my love stayed behind in Cambridge, it melted in the spring together with the deep snows, and by the summer, by the time of your arrival, only the scar remained—and hope, hope that you could bring it back to life. I should have figured this out sooner: bringing things back to life is not your métier.

An unexpected call from home—from a girlfriend who went into business about a year ago and the only one of all

my Kyiv friends and acquaintances who can afford to call
the States: "Are you sitting down, are you able to handle
some really terrible news?" she asks. "Like what?" There
is a short pause in the receiver and then a choked voice:
"Darka's dead." One second and my legs feel like they've
just been blasted with hot ash and go numb, and right
after that my whole body loses feeling, like anesthesia:
No! (But somewhere in the back of my mind buzzes a
nasty thought, like an escaped insect on a windowpane:
lucky dog, her suffering's over—because she did suffer
really a lot, beautiful, smart, she looked so good in those
colorful peasant kerchiefs she would tie back, with tassels
over the shoulders of her sheepskin coat—rosy cheeks,
high cheekbones, like a dark-red winter apple, a sharp,
mouse-like nose, heart-shaped lips, a genuine artifact of
folklore, a living illustration to Gogol's "Christmas Eve,"
and she had a great sense of humor, also Gogolian, classic
Ukrainian: the type where you're spinning your tale deadly
serious and the audience is on the floor laughing—and
yet her whole youth was one of suffering—with her stupid
mother who screwed up both her husband and her kids,
with her asshole men: her first husband left her as soon as
he graduated, as soon as he was assigned to a job in the
capital, which was the reason, it turned out, that he married her in the first place; her second marriage ended in
a terminated pregnancy and after that there was no end
to gynecological problems, straight downhill; and with
her third man, mushy as Wonder Bread and always unem-
ployed, she had to work for two while he looked after the
kid, at least he did that much—she tutored all the private
students she could get, accepted translations, hopped

around from one rental unit to another the way we all did, pulling her family behind her on her back, completed her dissertation, and wonder of wonders finally got a job in some newly established Ukrainian-American foundation, got on her feet about three months ago, they were driving back from Boryspil airport—a stone-drunk Lada toward them in their lane, head-on collision: four people, everybody in the car, dead on the spot, good-bye Charlie, and only a high, thin clear voice laments—tearlessly!—like a soundtrack to a film: "oh had I known I'd be dying, I'd have asked you to cut down the sycamore, to build a casket of four sides strong, so it would stand there thirty-four years long, it stood there, it stood there, and began to rot, and the casket turned to the girl and began to talk: either burn me up, or chop me up, either chop me up—or give the body up ") Standing in the middle of the kitchen with the receiver in my hand, holding on to Sana's voice asking for the tenth time what will happen to Talia now, what will happen—Talia's only five, high cheekbones, looks a lot like her mother, nice-looking except for her father's potato nose, one time when she was still an infant she had struck you with her lost, wavering, questioning, watery look in her eye, which seemed to be searching for something to fix itself to—Darka was changing her diaper, and suddenly this poem appeared, whispered by an invisible wind:

> How strange it is—a girl, a child.
> An expression of dissatisfaction on her face:
> First straighten out this life,
> Then call me in.
> You little doll, you tiny person, forgive—

A world who-knows-when painted last,
Your parents, who threw you in here
As though to your death on a barren field
—Okay, start growing!

—standing this way she distinctly hears that *other*, sound-track voice—not Darka's, although Darka was a good singer and Ukrainian folk-songs she did particularly well, who knows where she got that natural, chesty, folk intonation—a deep, precipitous wellspring—you can't fake that if you don't have it, even the most drunken crowd would melt, curling back in their chairs like tripe, just as soon as Darka took a deep puff of her cigarette—tilting her brow: "nicotine-vitamine"—and began to sing in that incredibly clear voice, her face would clear up with a gentle sadness, flower petals fell to the ground, horses stood quietly, ears perked, boats swayed from side to side in the waves at the shore, splish-splash, splish-splash, splish-splash, grass rustled under someone's stealthy steps, and the water carried away willow leaves; and everything else, all over the world, was carried away by water, some kind of nameless people populated this world, they yearned for something, they loved and they suffered, and only the scattered wet traces of voices (wails?) were left in their wake—you can only drink from those tiny tracks, you can only feel: that your own suffering, illuminated for an instant by a late, setting ray of meaning—is not the only one out there, not the first nor the last, and suddenly she remembers that in the song with the casket it actually stood empty for *twenty*-four rather than *thirty*-four years: that woman, who sang about her death in such high and piercing tones (I'd lay down my husband, but I love him so, I'd lay down myself, but my child is small: lie down, my dear wife, your child will be fine, people will help out…) was in fact a lot younger than us, still a kid—and you (that's Sana railing at me now), have you gone mad out there, you idiot, making a huge tragedy out of a bad fuck—well, if you put it *that* way, then it's not really a tragedy, everything depends on how you tell the story, except that Sana doesn't know, and nobody knows what Darka told you shortly before you left—that was perhaps the first time she really opened up to you even though you'd known each other since college, a year earlier Darka's father had died—he was an award-winning musician, a deputy, and in his day practically a member of the Communist Party Central Committee, although, it's true, even he got into a little trouble for "nationalism," so he started playing at state concerts, while his wife, who had gotten used to a comfortable life, would nag him to death if ever he tried to give a toast at official banquets in Ukrainian—even if uttered thickly and stupidly, playing the jester with his "howdy-doody" wordplays, the Central Committee official representative—a concrete slab in a gray suit—sat disapprovingly silent: not a single muscle moved on his impenetrable, seemingly waterlogged, face, ai-ai-yai, we're in trouble now, "and you were gonna go on that trip to Canada," the wife yelped, taking off her coat in the hall while a pregnant Darka, dying from the toxicity, was grinding up some coffee in the kitchen for her father— "you use that head of yours for thinking, ever?"—and her old man, after walking into the kitchen and lighting up a cigarette (first breaking a few matches), told his daughter roughly (also, like his wife, in Russian): "I know, I'm merely a sociopolitical buffoon," and this phrase stayed with her always, a hammered-in nail—she buried him at the exclusive Baikove cemetery, obituaries in all the papers, and the orchestra played, according to the wishes of the deceased, the Cossack farewell—"the stallion bowed his head," the late child, Darka was a late child, by the time she was born her father was forty, a good-looking, mature man at the height of his fame, how else could you hang on to him if not with another child?—"I've just now, myself a woman, understood my mother," Darka told you with pain in her eyes, "I just got it—I'm the one who shows up at the end of the banquet and pays the bill"—that night she didn't sing and the two of you huddled at the end of the table and you listened, chilled to the marrow by the blast of brutal courage with which she confronted life, and equally by the bone-piercing draft of at-once established sisterhood: we pay, girls, we do, we pay for everything, down to the last penny!—then we were flagging down a cab, cramming inside like sardines, crackling the thick cellophane of our flower bouquets: it was somebody's birthday, maybe even Sana's—someone was trying to squeeze in between the seats, somebody in an awkward fur coat was squeezing onto someone's lap, giddy-up!—as the first Soviet cosmonaut apparently said—and—you were off, in flight, two sisters, two doves: you across the ocean, and Darka—further still, a milk-white shadow setting out from a pile of crushed metal and on to one of the most distant stars—late child, brought into the world by a mother who wanted to hang on to her husband, and once there was no one to hang on to—life was exhausted, God opened his right hand and released the aching soul: peace be with you, tormented one, go and rest.

Darka, dear. Darka, can you hear me?

It was not your fault that you were called into this world by something other than love. Pray, wherever you are out there, for all of us—we still have to go on living.

Waking up in the morning (what for?), she lies on her stomach for a long time: the new day pours into her mind with a hail of exhausting and senseless obligations—order Xeroxes for her students, run off another term test on the departmental copier, stop off at the bank, the drugstore—she's run out of vitamins, and it wouldn't hurt to get some more panty hose, answer two letters, call the travel agency, oh God!—her ticket to New York, the one that was to be mailed to her, has somehow gotten lost, although, if you think about it, she needs New York now like a hole in the head—so she'll get herself out on stage, so she'll read in English the two or so poems that were translated with such huge effort, so she'll drink a glass of wine standing up and swallow down a few shrimp dipped in tomato sauce, grin at two or three neatly ironed literary agents and some gentlemen from the PEN Club, perhaps will pop in for an hour or two to her once-beloved museums (*"The fuck I need those museums for,"* he hollered happily into the phone calling her in Cambridge, still from Ukraine, *"the only thing I need to see in all of that America there is one dame!"*—at the time it seemed like bravado: how can you consciously refuse something, cut off your life at the stump, when it's so immeasurably interesting!—but now, look how she herself has lost all taste for exploration, her former insatiable, all-absorbing desire to discover something new—holy shit, am I dead already or what?...The first conversation they had on the subject turned out kind of stupid: *"I'm going to America—will you go with me?"*—*"Sure,"* he was laughing, *"by car, as long as the diesel lasts."*—*"I'm serious."*—*"What will I do there?"* You'll paint, you dork, you'll see the Metropolitan, and the Museum of Modern Art, and the Art Institute in Chicago, the mirrored octahedrons, the cosmic, gigantic stalagmites that gather on the horizon as you drive up to the city, the arched breathing of the bridges and viaducts over the expressways, space from a fantasy film or a dream, terrifying and endless, there's no stopping it, the open expanse, prairies without the cowboys, a light taste of madness, which flickers among the nighttime flashes of billboards: the mind, frightened of its own creation, because this civilization is entirely man-made and that's why you've got the somnambulant's aching longing of the saxophone, poured like the light of the moon over the desert, the reeling [black man drunk in the middle of the sidewalk] voice of a jazz-club singer, which pulls your soul out of your body with each languorous twist: "I'm all alone in this big city— Wilson, buddy, have some pity," cigarette smoke undulating in the duskiness over the bar, over the billiard tables and the sound of cue sticks striking the balls, we are all alone here, free and alone, it's wonderful—to build your life on your own, it's frightening—to build your life on your own, you'll see up close the faces of all the races brought together, the hues and tints—from melted chocolate [how shamelessly mauve are the shells of lips in the nakedness of their lining, how beastlike the distension of the nooks of nostrils!] to Asian chimera greenish tint—yellow moon, lemon, unripe avocado—all this is mixed in one crucible, what a wild film, deafening to the eyes, there's no stopping it, colorful tents on the street like at a county fair, the chrysolite luster of display windows in broad daylight, and over all of that, on the billboards—bright caramel, smiling, several-meter-high faces of killed children: victims of "drunk driving," little angels of this whole earthly valley of tears rising up to heaven, O Davey, O Kevin, O Mary Jane, where will we all be tomorrow?—you'll see the sun setting over the Atlantic from the airplane window: it sinks rapidly, before your eyes, casting a bright-red path along the horizon, and snows of cloud gloam into limestone, into the rock of dark veins of ravines and then begin to break up, like ice on a river, into gray torsos of cooled steel-blue melted patches; only in the spot where the sun has sunk can you still make out a sharply defined island of glowing embers, but the ocean fog is already rolling in from all directions and the airplane enters the night, passing through it from end to end in about an hour, and now once again you see a little gray out the window, this time dawning—you will feel the planet breathing—like the pulsing soft crown of a newborn infant, it's so close to God up there in the sky, because as we lift off and break out of our comfortable burrows, we open up to him the same way as when we are born or die—and you will break out, I believe it, I know it!—you will break out of the blind alley through which, like a stubborn fool, you persist in crawling toward your hospital-prison-lobotomy [and what the fuck is this self-indulgence anyway, boys—is despair not too great a luxury for Ukrainians who, after all, were granted for the first time this century a realistic chance of leading a full life?...], you will paint your greatest paintings, and fame— *real* fame, the kind that no Ukrainian has yet achieved save perhaps Archipenko—will lead you—perhaps the first among us—into the blinding light of the projector of history, because you are worth more than their Shemiankin or even Neizvestnyi, because you truly are "such a damned good painter," and it is *you* who deserve to have your own gallery in Soho, it must be out there somewhere waiting for you while you're ruining your eyes every night there in your miserable little studio with no running water, where plaster from the ceiling falls on your just-made sculptures, I am so sick of this classic national defeatism—can't take any more!—we'll hustle about, we'll search around asking for the "right people," they'll be able to see your stuff, this is just the right time, after all, there is a "Ukraine," such as it is, art managers are beginning to look for new names, everything will be great, we'll do it, God, I want so much for us to finally *see* something, for someone to finally *hear* us, and how much effort I've put into this business—effort down the drain, I can't bear to think of it! dragging out West the most select books and slides from home, sticking them under people's noses, pretending with smoke-and-mirrors around me that there's some kind of illusory context to all this, waving my arms around all the lecterns—the stunned director of the Kennan Institute assured me afterward in a thank-you letter that "if the fate of Ukrainian literature is in the hands of people like yourself, one need not fear for its future"—not suspecting, of course, that the only thing in my hands is perhaps the handrail on a bus, and only if they push me away from that as well—it's okay, bro, no worries, we'll break out, I'll pull, drag you out on my back, I'll have enough strength for all of it: bring half of Ukraine to its feet, bring half of America over to Ukraine to take a look [and she really did pass over their continent like some kind of Pied Piper: students from her classes would sign up for the Peace Corps practically en masse—asking for "Ukraine," colleagues from American universities began studying Ukrainian, flywheels of audacious projects would start up—joint publications, symposia, translated anthologies, good God, how many minds did she pollute!]—and to all of her inspired exhortations he would only give a wry smile: well-well, "*We'll see*"; that "we'll see" of his with time began to sound like a password for hopelessness, at first she would discount such lack of faith as a sign of provincial insecurity: it's not for folks like us— "*No, I would still like to hear you explain to me, how you could just—disappear like that, without a word, without a sign?*" he'd bristle, eyes open wide: "*I'm telling you, I didn't believe I'd ever be coming here!*"—well, so now you've come, and what did you get out of it, since you already knew so well in advance that "the fuck you needed all this for"? He brought that thick album with his drawings and he used it for all his paintings here: all those same little men with shaved heads and sharp features carrying on their spears, over hills through an orange desert, either moon-green large-eyed fish, or a gigantic forefinger of the left hand [why *left?*], or an embroidered banner fluttering in the wind, they were suspended between the flaming sky and the darkening earth, their childish, narrow bare feet walking on the jagged wheels of a grinding machine: this is how, he slyly squinted his eyes at her, God teaches poets to walk—she snorted in disagreement, or rather, in half disagreement: who knows, maybe it's really so?). How, *based on what* does he continue to paint, if the world around him is uninteresting? You're an unfortunate man, Mykola: you loved a car and you crashed it, you loved a woman and you broke her—on the night of their final breakup she dreamed (and this dream she actually remembered, carried it out of the darkness) that he was slowly walking away, back toward her—the back of his head with that spiky hair still so dear to her, his head lowered, shorts and well-starched white shirt with short, stiff sleeves sticking out: always the tough guy!—walking along a narrow plank heading *down* somewhere, where—she couldn't tell, and calmly (for the first time in all the days spent with him—calmly!), lucidly, and matter-of-factly the realization came in her sleep: he won't be saved, nope, he won't.

But you, girlfriend, look like shit, oh boy, you really look like shit: at least forty, even after you went out and got your hair cut (she had mustered all her strength for this heroic deed, because her condition was such, especially in the evenings, that one time she almost fell asleep still in her clothes and only the strangely conscious pang of fear through the sticky haze of her heavy brain—what is this, have I lost it totally?!—forced her finally to lower her legs to the floor, feel around for her bathrobe, change, and stumble to the bathroom: don't forget your makeup, with a cotton ball, that's it, dip it into the lotion, wipe under your eyes, now brush your teeth, first gargling with Listerine, excellent, good girl, and now into the shower!—and now, okay, here we go, nice rubdown with the towel, nighttime Oil of Olay, there's the black box on the shelf, first the neck, then the face, pat-pat, with fingertips, massage it a bit, good, done, don't forget, lid back on the jar—and now you're all set to go to bed, everything in order)—and all that effort as much good as hot compresses for a corpse: unexpectedly emerging to meet herself in one of those full-length mirrors, whether in a store or on the street, she at first wouldn't recognize this hag in familiar, elegant outfits, and it wasn't just the frightening skin, suddenly aged by several years (you should really smoke less…) and blotched with remnants of pimples, and not even the flaccid outline of the bottom half of her face, like a balloon that had lost air (get ready to hear a bunch of whining the minute someone with a face like that opens her gob!), but this now: here's something new—something had imperceptibly changed in her whole posture, her gestures, her walk: that unrestrained drive of an airplane gathering momentum for take-off that had always been within her was gone, and, removing her tinted glasses she looked closer: yes, her eyes had lost their spark—they no longer leapt from her face like projector lights, but rather hid in it with such tearstained sorrow that she herself couldn't wait to avert her glance elsewhere. They say that according to statistics a person looks into the mirror forty-three times a day—forty-three times you, squeezed by deep fear and still not quite believing it, stare at this Megaera aghast: so this is me? From now and forever? (And immediately the tears well up, this time from hopelessness, a forgotten feeling from adolescence.) Hmm, yeah, this is bad. No wait, if you changed the lighting, take it from above and at a slight angle it wouldn't be quite so bad, there's still something of that old me showing through... Oh, please!—whom are you kidding? Last winter still, during that flight through Frankfurt when she was sitting curled up by the wall and fervently writing something down in her notepad, reeling with invisible pain—packs of young men walking by would slow down with curiosity, trying to strike up a conversation: "Hi, girl!"; only a year ago in Cambridge a super stud was pursuing her, good-looking and an athlete, six foot two and about that much across the shoulders, too, gentle as a baby rabbit, with skin like dark silk and the smell of a healthy young man, ah, what a lover he would have been—you can wring your hands now, go ahead, and to her "I'm ten years older than you," he replied after a pause, surprised, "You're lying"—for him, too, she was, sincerely and simply, a "girl" he liked— while for her, rather than being seductive, that invincible force of ignorant health, that happy and confident *inexperience with real pain* was secretly irritating, because she was, after all, "a poetess of acutely tragic sensibility," as one dull-witted critic had written back home, oh yeah, she had inherited it the way she inherited her blood type, and in this country with its code of compulsory happiness, which, it goes without saying, produces thousands upon thousands of neurotics and psychopaths, she carried her historical suffering like an act of defiance, like a blue ribbon from a pedigree dog show—with an ever so slight smile of superiority she would speak to trustingly open mouths (her words fell into raised glasses of wine and rippled their glimmering surfaces): in your culture tragedy is of an exclusively personal character, loneliness, love dramas,

those clinical incests that forty-year-old matrons supposedly dig out from their childhood memories in psycho-
therapeutic séances, and which I, truth be told, don't
particularly believe—after a year or two of psychiatric sessions you'll start recalling a lot more than that—however,
you are unfamiliar with subjugation to limitless, metaphysi-
cal evil, where there's absolutely nothing in hell you can
do—when you grow up in a flat that is constantly bugged
and surveilled and you know about it, so you learn to speak
directly to an invisible audience: at times out loud, at times
with gestures, and at times by saying nothing, or when the
object of your first girlish infatuation turns out to be a
fellow assigned to spy on you, who after a year of rather
poorly performed duties—generally conversations in cafes
and hanging out at the movies—suddenly falls in love with
you for real, no joking, and confesses his love—at the same
time confessing his KGB mission (the mouths open wider
yet, rounder: now that's life, they think jealously, that's
"real life"!), and there's more, there's more—but actually
she prefers be silent on this matter—when at age thirty
you first hop into bed with a foreigner, an overwhelmingly
romantic act of passion (with an amazingly pleasant smell
of expensive deodorant!), which he, regardless, took seriously and even began to say something about marriage—it
was your luck in life, girl, to keep picking up serious guys,
no matter which—each wanted to get married right away,
some kind of disease, or something? a marriage epidemic,
or was it perhaps a fashion trend for poetesses?—and that
sweet-smelling (and gentle, oh yeah!) man tried to get you
an entire wardrobe, because your own comprised an old
pair of jeans and a few, no longer bohemian, already rather

ragged tops—he bought you two *real* dresses of fine wool, and a silvery silk blouse with shoulder pads, and a gorgeous suit the color of red wine in which you instantly ignited in a glow of a now completely alien exotic beauty (swimming pools, lounge chairs, yachts, white sports cars...), and several pairs of shoes (big hello from Gogol's Vakula—Italian, one-hundred-dollar pumps of the softest leather, which you still wear to this day), and a whole pile of accessories, a little purse, and a butterfly swarm of colorful scarves, and makeup, and resonant gypsy bangles, a watchband to emphasize yet again the artistic narrowness of your wrist and rich, dangling earrings to do the same for your thin, vulnerable neck; everything was expensive, chosen lovingly and with taste—and, for the first time in your life supplied to gills, for the first time dressed up like in a glossy magazine, so that you yourself lost your breath when you looked into the mirror (and ditto for each of the forty-three times!)—you sank into unbearable, burning *shame*, you felt yourself a typical Soviet whore who screws in a hotel room for a few pairs of underwear, and although *not to accept* all those goods turned out to be more than you were able, but with that the affair came to an end—you simply stopped answering his calls from Amsterdam (and in the meantime he was quickly filing for his divorce, or perhaps even did file), because, when all's said and done, what would there have been for you to do in Amsterdam?—and you went back to your husband, bringing back jeans and cigarette lighters for him from your trips abroad, and you might not have been exactly satisfied, but you were *clean*: maybe relations weren't perfect, but they were *human*, not beset from the beginning by the humiliating inequality of nations and circumstances that were beyond your control (and that's why in the States she was not at all concerned that her great love lived off her paycheck: "big deal," you'll make some money, you'll pay me back—it only got to her, and in no small measure—that was when she broke down, started running around the house, tumbling for a few hours into the pit of black, fiery, burning-in-the-gut hatred, ready herself, like his former wife, to hurl at him, should he happen to appear, all present knives and other stabbing and cutting objects, so that he'd come crashing down, the bastard, dripping with blood, so that he'd shit blood, so he'd come blood!—aaarrgh, disgusting, thank you kindly for these emotional experiences, would have much rather never known this about myself!—it only got to her when, with his chilling arrogant implacability—after all, he's a man! a rock!—he announced, already over the telephone, that he owes her nothing—that actually it's quite the opposite, that it's she who still owes him—no kidding, he must've tallied up some penalty charges—for those bricks, for none other than those bricks!—and although it sounded like a threat, she gave a raspy laugh, still not quite believing it: "*So listen, will I have to get the mob after you?*"—but by that time he had already hung up—real hero, good boy, charming!—raving mad in her rage, she was gently held back by the shoulder by a fleeting thought: it must be so f-fucking miserable to live this way—regularly evoking these kinds of responses from people, and not only from women!—how unhappy he must be, the idiot, and he won't even go see a doctor...). "Do you know the Ukrainian night," ladies and gentlemen? Nah, you know fuck-all about the Ukrainian night, and there's nothing in it for you to know, you've got your own, no less turbid nights, you commit suicide in elegant, suburban, ivy-covered homes because there's nobody to eat turkey with for Thanksgiving, it's just that I've had it with my own universal empathy, I've had it because, you see, no matter which way I turn, there's misery, misery, and misery—maybe that's the way I'm wired, or maybe it's my "acutely tragic sensibility" always picking up the odor of misery like an insect's antennae, and groaning, I crawl toward it rather than happily screwing my young, healthy stud (who, incidentally, led astray by me, has gone on to, wonder of wonders, start reading—he's already polished off *Uncle Tom's Cabin*, something from Jane Austen, and has now settled on *Tom Sawyer*, and then one evening while drinking tea in my kitchen—he used to drop by after the gym, rosy-red, pull his jacket off over his head, and throw it on the bed, he had a funny way of smelling his shoulders like a puppy dog: just back from the pool, still smell like chlorine—it was life that he smelled like, damn it, life!—he related with some excitement that he had already learned to *picture* the landscape described in a given book, or the room, and suddenly he interrupted himself and asked simple-heartedly: where was he supposed to now find a girl that he'd be able to discuss all this with?—oh, you clever boy, bull's-eye, right with the very first step: the path she was opening up to him promised— loneliness—it hit her like a slap in the face: stop, you idiot, hit the brakes—will you finally stop fucking up the minds of young men, pushing them toward the deceptive lights of some kind of deeper meaning, which you yourself have no clue about, and afterward abandoning them halfway to lick their wounds for the next few years?—and she already knew that she wouldn't be sleeping with him, that it would be only with someone as screwed up as herself, no, far more screwed up—in a plaster cast, with draconian debts and trails of police summonses, my sorcerer-brother, we are of the same blood you and I—whom she'd be unable to throw off his own God-given track—oh, how noble of you, sweetness, just look at yourself, just look at how well you've done—all-round good girl, no?). In psychiatry, I believe it's called victim behavior, but there's nothing I can do about it, it's the way I was taught; and in general all that Ukrainians can say about themselves is how, and how much, and by which manner they *were beaten*: information, I must say, not very enticing for strangers, nonetheless, if there's nothing else in either your family or your national history that can be scraped together, we slowly but surely began to take pride in this—hey, come see how they beat us, but we're not yet dead—my Cambridge friends rolled on the ground with laughter when you translated the beginning of your national anthem as "Ukraine has not died yet"— "What kind of anthem is that?"—and truly, a pretty screwed up little opening line, just the thing to "go fight the Turk" with, like hell!—and that's why, that's why, my dear girl, since that's the case—you should shout and rejoice that you haven't died, you poor sexual victim of the national idea, although, if you think about it some, there's not a whole lot to be rejoicing about, and who needs it, a life without love, and wouldn't it be preferable to die, or even better, to never be born than now go through such torture? (Once upon a time I had a certain, oh so excellently programmed patriotic friend who constantly complained about the fact that we fall in love not with the man, but with the national idea—and in the end, after a several-year excursion through the bedrooms of overseas grandpas, she finally settled down in one of them, having acquired a *bébé*—which, it's not out of the question, might even learn to speak Ukrainian when it grows up, that's if it wants to, of course, and meantime its mom is making a few bucks preparing news reports for the Ukrainian service of Radio Liberty, which Clinton still hasn't decided whether to shut down—chirping away in her once-native tongue with those foreign intonations sticking out like springs from a mattress and designed to show that she is now a cut above—no longer from the home village: she **broke out!**): I'm making the point, ladies and gentlemen, that it's not such a great thrill to belong to a beaten nation, as the fox in the folktale said, the unbeaten rides on the back of the beaten—and that's what the beaten one deserves, the problem is that in the meantime that beaten one manages to sing, let's say, the ballad of the misfortunate captives, and in this way— legitimizes his own humiliated position, because art, don't you know, always legitimizes, in the eyes of an outsider, the life that gave it birth; and in that fact lies its, that is, art's, gre-eat deception. The Latin *ars*, which seeped into most European languages, the Nordic *Kunst*, which ricocheted over to our West Slavic neighbors as *sztuka*—now there's a healthy attitude, you can almost hear the after-dinner burp of a burgher's pickled cabbage: *sztuka*, a game, a trick, an acrobatic somersault on the tightrope, a melodic bell tone of a baroque clock, and a whimsically carved snuffbox; and our art, *mystetstvo*, or craftsmanship, is also of the same order. It's only with an indifferent condescending yawn— well, well, and what will the *craftsmen* entertain us with today?—that one can break that spell, neutralize it, expose the hidden trap, and, it seems, only Old Church Slavonic raises in vain its dried-out cautionary forefinger: beware *izkusstvo,* from *izkus*—temptation, the same you pray not to be led into.

There's just one thing, she tells herself, looking into the mirror for the four hundred and forty-third time (so this is it, for the rest of my life?)—the mirror is cloudy, with moldy-green spots (what do you expect from a cheap apartment in a poor neighborhood)—at her face, crudely touched-up by approaching old age (thirty-four years old, no fucking joke!). Just one. They never taught us, all our literature with its entire cult of tragic love—Ivanko and Marichka, Lukash and Mavka, my students were enthralled and declared *Forest Song* superior to *Midsummer Night's Dream,* you bet—they somehow forgot to warn us that in reality tragedies *don't look pretty.* That death, no matter what form it takes, is first and foremost an ugly business. And where there's no beauty—how can there be truth?

It's too bad. It's too damned bad. Should I head out to the balcony for a smoke?

A discovery: this is how frigid women see the world! There was a time—the last few days of living together and right after the breakup—when, on seeing an erotic scene on television, she would start to cry. Now she watches calmly, like a zoologist watching lizards copulate (hmm, I wonder, how do lizards do it?): two half-naked people in bed, the man places his hand on the woman's thigh, moves it up, she turns toward him, her legs, bent at the knees, spread; she throws her arms around his neck and the two of them, moaning and tussling about, melt into a kiss...Thank God, next scene.

She had once blurted out, without thinking, in a so-called shared moment of an interesting confidential observation: *"You know? Just don't misunderstand me, don't be offended: it seems to me that you're open to evil."* That was about the third or fourth day after his arrival in the Pennsylvania boon-docks where the good-hearted Mark is happy to invite, at the expense of his department, all the poets and artists of the whole world at the same time, if only they would help him escape the storms of hell at home for an hour or two (every time he called her in Cambridge he related, in a voice that would go well with a bird's tilted head: cuck-oo: "Today I met a lovely little Russian girl," "There's a black girl here kind of interested in me"—who'd be interested in the poor thing, an awkward forty-year-old schoolboy with excellent grades, with his duck's waddle, the tummy of a teddy bear, nose-hairs showing, and thinning hair on his crown—and then he'd return again to his home life with the intonations of a hurt child: today he had to do all the dishes and was late to work because of it, and the only thing *she* could say was that the frying pan wasn't done right—the intonations would jump into shrieking hysteria when, having exhausted all possible ways of consoling him, she asked plainly, "Mark, if it's all so hopeless, then why haven't you split up?"—"Because the fucking bitch couldn't survive!"—aha, the house bills, the "mortgage," the "insur-ance," and all other maintenance, it's a good thing we in Ukraine don't have such problems, a lot simpler for us, you pack your bags, slam the door, and "good-bye, my love": poverty is freedom is freedom)—Mark arranged for a studio for him over the summer holidays: a corner in a huge barn, kind of like a surreal-looking gym crammed with easels, with a frosted-glass window the kind you have in bathrooms extending the full length of the wall—you should be grateful to him for that, fella, beggars can't be choosers—she herself had come to that empty university town only for him, it was for him she left Cambridge, and as soon as she did it was like a wall had been hit by a battering ram and come tumbling down, everything shifted from its place: already in Boston's Logan airport, as soon as she got out of the taxi her sandal strap broke—dragging her foot she walked up to the check-in counter to find out that all United flights were delayed, Washington, where she was to transfer to the mangy Pennsylvania turbo-prop, was in the grips of a thunderstorm—she started running around from one customer agent to another, all shot back empty smiles like flyswatters, what could she do, she absolutely had to be at Mark's house tonight because they were heading out by car to New York the next morning, to Kennedy airport to meet the brilliant Ukrainian artist who doesn't (idiot!) speak a word of English, the script was prepared so well, and now this screwup!—she was able to get on another flight, sweating on the plane for forty minutes to elevator music in her headphones (interrupted every five minutes by cheerful promises of departure just as soon as they receive permission), and at Dulles it was like war had been declared moments earlier: people thundered down the corridor, bags bouncing across their shoulders, carts squealed, wheels screaked, an invisible child was bawling along the entire length of the corridor's rafters, and she, too, charged after the others, from one level to another, looping around like in a nightmare or horror film, from gate to gate, and when she finally ran up, panting like a race dog, to the isolated corner with the gate for her turbo-prop, she crashed right into the proverbial immovable mountain, a professionally pleasant clerk behind the counter: "Your plane has just left, ma'am"—so when's the next one?—oh the next one is tomorrow at noon—he flashed his teeth: "Have a good night!"—she swore up and down, tried to phone Mark, all the telephone booths were jammed, the machine ate up her quarter, the angry hordes at the United counters were going crazy, demanding their rights (here's where you see the difference between us and Americans), a huge man with a full shock of hair, for some reason wet, who was clearly on the verge of an epileptic attack, was violently shaking a black man in a United uniform with an also shiny-wet face: "You're a jerk, you hear me, man? You go and bring me your boss right now, you hear? Right now!"— the fellow, with the whites of his eyes bulging, struggled to get away, slurring and spraying: "You just don't call me names!"—and pulling the radio receiver out of his pocket with the elegant gesture of a magician or perhaps a waiter he called, not the requested boss but rather the police, well, this you would have gotten in Sovietland as well—Rosie whined into the receiver that Mark had already left for the airport to meet her—outside the glass doors, in the yellow-lit darkness, she once again saw the diagonal spears of rain, she hobbled over to the baggage claim conveyer belts to pick up her bags since it was obvious now that she'd be spending the night in Washington, the small-built

baggage-handler with a pitted nose, like it had been trans-
ferred from someone else's face, eagerly informed her as
soon as he saw her claim stub that they had managed to
transfer the Boston bags to the damned turbo-prop *in
time*—they really had to hustle, ma'am, they only had ten
minutes, but they made it, thank God, don't worry, ma'am—
he stood there glowing with his accomplishment and
awaited praise, she almost felt bad about disappointing
him: you mean the luggage went on without me? I'm standing in an airport called Dulles in the city of Washington
on the continent North America on the planet Earth with
a ladies' purse over my right shoulder, in my left hand there
is a computer bag, no toothbrush, no spare set of underwear, at this moment flying over the Atlantic is a man for
whom I arranged this whole business, and yet this indeed
is—my only address: after collecting her thoughts somewhat
as she smoked two cigarettes in a row, she changed her
ticket yet again—destination JFK: if this is how things are
Mark can meet both of us there tomorrow, we'll each arrive
separately, but we'll find each other somehow; she called
some friends in Washington who had been inviting her to
come stay for quite some time, although probably not at
midnight and without warning—hi there, so I'm here, in
Dulles, "if you could just give me a drink of water, because
I'm so hungry I don't even have anywhere to stay," as the
saying goes—and this is the literally the case: with their
address written down on a scrap of paper—"it's a fifteen-
minute drive, we're waiting for you," phew, the world's not
without good people—feeling a smile of a mentally chal-
lenged child permanently glued to her face, no doubt from
fatigue, she shuffled off to the taxi stand, but this was not

yet the end: there was a tiny Pakistani at the wheel in whose coarsely grated speech English was not to be discerned so easily—bravely heading out into the night, at exactly fifteen minutes later he turned his head toward her in the darkness of the car—slowly, as if on hinges, headlights of approaching cars lapped back and forth like waves, like the shadows of giant invisible fish, the red tableau of the meter flickered like an abandoned cardiogram in an operating room where all the doctors have left—and he asked her, did she happen to know how to get there—excuse me, but isn't it the cab driver that's supposed to know the way?—the nakedness of empty suburban expressways, the blackness of the night on either side without a single light, where am I, Lord, who am I, why am I here?—another fifteen minutes and they drove into a town, they sped up neatly swept moonlit streets, first one way, then turning around, the other, how long have you been in the States?—she shouted at him from the back seat like he was deaf—five years, he answered, continuing to hold his head in the same awkward position—and he kept stopping his cab, and he kept turning on the light, and he kept pulling out the crumpled blanket of a map from under his seat, holding on to it with both hands like it was the magic carpet that would miraculously deliver us, and kept waiting for something as he stared at it, she thought dully for a moment that perhaps the poor guy didn't know how to read—what did you say the street was called?—he rolled the pebbles of disobedient syllables in his mouth unable to pronounce "Rupert Street," nor could he repeat them after her, because she *also* spoke with an accent, perhaps not as vigorous as his, "Kood yoo koll dereh?"—uh? aha, "could you call

there," in other words, to the place we've been trying to get
to for the second hour now, my friends are probably losing
their minds, she calls and then she disappears!—good,
hand over the receiver—once, twice, and a third time, at
first they couldn't get a connection, and then finally an
aggravated Ron (who, it turns out, had already been calling
the cab company), was giving the driver, who still could not
shake his ataraxy, some kind of multi-storied instructions,
and once again the speeding up and down empty streets
began, as though the driver had turned over all his senses
to car: the cab rushed and groaned desperately, stopped,
snorted, scratched the back of its head, and asked itself:
what if I go that way?—it cursed (squealing its wheels),
wrung its hands, and in the half darkness of the car interior
the Pakistani's silent *fear* slowly spread, she could sense it
physically—it was beginning to make her queasy, the man
was watching his job slip through his helpless hands like a
rope, his frail support in this freakish land, and devil take
this "ledi" with her strange accent who got it into her head
to go devil-knows-where in the middle of the night—she
felt bad, wanting to occupy less and less space in the back
seat, and after the fourth (!!!!) call "dereh" Ron was screaming into the phone: "Where are you? Stay where you are,
just don't move, man, okay?"—after five minutes a white
car flew out from around the bend, Ron's figure jumped
out, ripped open the door of the cab, your lungs filled with
the humid smell of a summer night, and into the car—Ron's
furious seething ("it's fifteen minutes' drive, man, you just
don't know your business!")—and crawling out to freedom,
swaying on her high heels (the left sandal had fallen apart
totally, could not be held together) she suddenly felt a wet

gurgle in her panties: her period had begun. End of paragraph.

And she could not muster up any pity for the Pakistani—he was too frightened to take any money, not a cent, well, too bad, he wasn't he only one who had a bad day...She fell asleep at Ron and Martha's with that same idiotic smile still attached to her face like cookie crumbs: well-well, it occurred to her as she fell asleep, my darling's on his way, he sure is—the catastrophes have begun raining down! So it's small wonder that her first reaction at the sight of her beloved man at Kennedy—he was standing against a wall, chattering away with fellow travelers on the Kyiv flight in the most innocent way, jeans jacket, the familiar gray spiky hair, she saw him before he saw her, how many times had she played out this scene in her mind!—was an involuntary prickle of hostility—whereas he, look at him, scampered toward her as fast as he could, planted a kiss on her cheek as though nothing much had happened, as though this half year of devastating waiting had never occurred, this futile burning of oil in the vessel of a vestal virgin, and there was no need for any explanations, behind him Mark bobbed up and down like an obedient penguin, his round belly protruding forward, well, true, this wasn't the time for long explanations, I'd like you to meet...—how dumb and inappropriate all this turns out to be, rumpled, chewed up, I'm simply tired, I have to rest, catch up on sleep, and he, too, has had a long flight, I'll figure it out later, later—and "later," once we got home, alone and face to face with each other, suitcases half-unpacked, it appeared—peeking out as if from afar, not quite yet accessing the still deadened, seared, gnawing instincts—that thought which she blurted out to him without thinking, brought it forward and laid it at his feet, like a dog retrieves a stick—*you know, it seems to me that you're open to evil.* He jumped back like someone stabbed him with a knife; that malevolent flame in his eyes was strange, she had seen it before—on the edge of a bared grin with sharply protruding incisors from under the upper lip, like it was *something else* that peered out for a moment through his narrow eyelids, red-rimmed and swollen from lack of sleep—it was late at night, they had stepped out for their first walk at the new place, to have a look at the neighborhood that mysteriously glimmered with colored lights in the yards and gardens; from the half-open doors of the single-story buildings bursts of music and laughter escaped from time to time, white T-shirts passed by in the gentle brown darkness, disappearing into its depths, the town was awake, in the throes of anticipation of a holiday: the annual arts festival would take place soon, look at that house straight out of Andersen's fairy tale, look at that interesting spire!—a new beginning, we will have a new beginning, *I still have to go light a candle in church—to thank God for helping me come here to be with you,* yes, yes, she nodded, all the horrors are behind us, all those fires, crushed cars and bodies, crazy flights, quite a story! there's only one thing to mention to keep in mind for later—*you know? Just don't misunderstand me, don't be offended: it seems to me that you're open to evil.* She was aiming, in the habit of a professional lecturing bore, to examine this issue further: it's not that the evil is actually lodged within you, but that you, in some fashion, manage to attract it—but there was no explaining:

he flashed a wild, otherworldly glare, just as they came out to an intersection—looked both ways and decidedly shook both his head and forefinger: that way!

And from that moment they were hopelessly lost.

Before that they had spent an hour wandering around their own, not-yet-accustomed-to abode (he was saying "our little house" as she was filled with the warmth of an inner smile)—time after time they would return to it and then set off in a different direction—when suddenly the whole neighborhood became unrecognizable, and they could not figure out which direction was home. Knocked off their bearings, they passed intersection after intersection, stoplight after stoplight, all their orientation points—the pseudo-Gothic spire, the hedge, the square with the trash bins, which they had walked by each time—vanished like into another dimension and after a few times she began asking directions (at least she remembered the address) from every passerby who crossed her path, of which there were fewer and fewer because it was already past midnight, tipsy students partying on the lawn of one of the yards simply shrugged their shoulders unable to say anything comprehensible but at the same time still managing to get into a fight discussing whether it should be left or right, and for quite some time after they had stupidly-smiling-sorry-apologized and taken off, they could still hear behind them the strident clamor of a female voice sliding over consonant clusters not very soberly—giving some Jerry hell for, as usual, not having a "damn clue" and naming the wrong street—they had obviously wandered off too far, it was actually quite funny—amused, she was translating the girl's scolding for him, poor Jerry—he, on the other hand, clammed up, demonstrating no such childish enthusiasm, but she still kept making fun of it, see, you should have listened to me, I've got a perfect sense of direction, it has never led me astray—yup, that much is true, sweetness, it's just that this time it was another one of your instincts that led you astray, fa-a-ar more important than mere direction. Did it ever.

This went on for about an hour—and then suddenly he stood stock-still and pointed: the hedge! They had been circling not more than several dozen yards away the whole time. Again the neighborhood "switched on," all the familiar landmarks bobbed up. How could they have been so blind, she wondered. That's right, "good question," as they are prone to saying around here. How could you have been so blind, you poor fool? So blinded at a time when everything around you was screaming, howling at you in direct speech? What's the panic, you would have tossed your head, no-oh, you would not have let it stop you, even if a fiery hand had appeared out of thin air and sketched a written warning on the wall right under your nose, you were in love, oh yes, you were sure that you *could do it* ("I can do anything!"), do what not a single person can do on their own for another—it can't be done, luv. It can't be done. Unless—and here, as they say in newspaper ads, different options are available—unless you exchange your own life for another's: exchange destinies. No, thank you very much, I had somewhat different plans for my life.

Too bad that they have now somehow altogether lost their meaning...

Their first night together, that mad—festival!—night with the crazy race toward the flashing avalanche of lanterns reflected in the street puddles, flying from one late-night pub to another, and finally to the completely unambiguous little bordello on the outskirts of town, who would have thought that they had something like this out in the provinces (unremarkable from the outside, except for all the expensive foreign cars—a house with two rooms "across the hall" from each other, in one room leather soles shuffled across the wooden floor, a densely compacted drunken human mass shoved to and fro in dance, and in the other, where they were served coffee and liqueur, there stood two cots covered with quite touching azure plaid blankets, over which hung some kind of obscene lithographs—"Kuprin! Straight out of Alexander Kuprin!"—she had burst out laughing; despite her physical exhaustion—it was her second night without sleep!—she was nonetheless very keenly aroused, like she had drunk champagne, by the pathetically exhibitionist theatricality of this atmosphere of cheap sin, by the convulsive music behind the thin wall, by the almost embarrassed look in the eye of the woman serving them drinks—she would especially remember seeing in the dance room a very young, scarcely eighteen-year-old prostitute with flowing chestnut-colored hair, attractive in that puppy-wet, bright, untarnished folk-song beauty that you can still find among girls in Volyhnia and Podillia—and the poor thing, dead drunk: "Listen"—she had latched on to them, sensing something out of the ordinary—"what's your name? My name is Maija. You're such a beaudiful cupple. Naawh, I'm seerious"—and when given a light for her cigarette she replied like a gracious girl, "Thank you kindly"—that local dialect "thank you kindly," just like they taught her at home!—for some reason pierced one to tears with an aching pitying tenderness: *"She's still a child and has no idea what's happening to her"*—she shared her feelings with him in the car on the way back—he shrugged his shoulders—*"Who the hell cares? She's just a wipe, that's all,"* and yet that "wipe" was the first to recognize the growing, awakening love between them, every love needs witnesses at its beginning, it needs—parental, tender approval from the outside world of this newly emerged union of two, and the world is never miserly in dispensing its blessing with warm, misty eyes, with the smiles with which old men turned to look at us in the train station café into which we brought from the street, in a flying, dancing rhythm, the fresh breeze of an invisible carnival, the atmosphere of sly glances at each other, little games, conspiratorial chortles over something frightfully funny but incomprehensible to anyone else—shining sequins, generously scattered lucky confetti, which, as it falls, slowly twirls in the air long after the door shuts behind the radiant couple, *"Which cigarette lighter do you want?"*—*"The red one"*—he turns to the bartender, spreading his arms helplessly like a comedian: *"She said—red"*—and the bartender begins to glow like a juicy peach, a smile washing over his face, he's a participant, and, filling the tall glasses with sticky, amber liquid, he lets it spill over the top—ah the world loves lovers, because only they, in the dull monotony of daily life, give it a sign that it's really different, better, than it's used to thinking of itself, that it's enough to stretch out your hand, twist the dial, and everything around begins to sparkle, glitter with the colorful lights of a child's kaleidoscope, begins to laugh

from an overabundance of strength, and breaks into a
dance!—the old street photographer on the park bench,
beside him a matron like a Scythian statue in a cloth pad-
ded jacket: "Photograph those young ones over there!"—
"Oh stop," he drones slowly, almost dreamily, "they've got
other things on their mind, they're in Love"—the last word
is spoken with a capital letter, and you, exchanging glances,
turn and rush over to be photographed, eager to either
offer yourself as a gift to these oldsters or, on the contrary,
thank them for the unexpected blessing that descended
like a wet kiss of a fallen leaf on your forehead—then he
takes away those photos and you will never see them again,
it's not impossible that he's already torn them to bits,
thrown them into the ashtray and set fire to them—afterward carefully pushing the ashes into a little pile with his
crooked baby finger—okay, darling, I've nothing against
it, you can engage in a little suffering, too: it was time for
you, too, at the tender age of forty-plus years, to discover
that not all of us are "wipes" or, in the best-case scenario,
"mousy loves," I'm sorry, but I only know how to play for
keeps, and if I'm not going to be your love, not a mousy
one but a real one, then I sure as hell won't be, in any way,
your "wipe": I prefer to be sandpaper, sir)—that first night,
it was probably then, in those moments of heightened
emotion, that somewhere deep inside her was born a
slightly ironic, sneering coldness: it's a fuck party and nothing more, with all the attendant attributes, like some off-
stage screenwriter had taken care to maintain the purity
of the genre (and moreover, as quickly became apparent,
a rather unsuccessful fuck party at that!)—however, they
don't call us gifted kids with enormous creative potential

for nothing, we can convert an unsuccessful fuck into a tragic love in a flash, driving ourselves into a totally suicidal state in the process—it was only after nine (that's right, nine!) months, in another land on another continent, on the night of the final fight in a room of some hillside motel—first tiptoeing around, smoking on the wooden veranda, they wrestled in hushed voices so as not to wake anyone up, then they went out walking—speaking at full volume as though the raising of voices meant automatically setting feet in motion—across the parking lot, between automobiles whose walrus sides flashed reflections of the moon, a stop—a confrontation, eye to eye—a spark!—a clash of sabers!—and suddenly he's turned around and running across the whole lot back to the room to pack his things, a small, almost waxlike figure in shorts quickly moving its naked legs—within him twirled, like a screw—it seemed as though you could hear it grinding—nothing but rallied pride, a burning fear of what, God forbid, "people might say" (the good old provinces talking, Khvylovy might have sighed!) if they were to learn that it was *she* who left him, yanked him out of his home turf, carried him over the ocean and dumped him, what a tough broad! they'd say, and that's why, heaving a travel bag quickly stuffed with his crap over his shoulder (*"Don't forget your sponge, dear,"* she was handing it to him from behind, now that she too had made it back to the room) he barked with that especially brutal, quarrelsome voice that he'd been in a habit of addressing her with lately: *"I'm flying home tomorrow! Thanks much for America!"* (she ha-ha-ha'd in her soul, despite not really being in a laughing mood, knowing full well that he wouldn't be flying anywhere, that by tomorrow or no later than the day after—a creative personality, after all!—he'd find himself some new version of his being here, in no way connected to her, which is exactly what happened)—and he tore off into the night—two and a half miles! with his stuff!—to that damned studio (I wonder if it's at least open at night or whether he'll just sit somewhere under a bush, crazy man, until morning?)—it was only then, after she closed the door after him, with mixed feelings about a show that wasn't quite over, a burning rod of "what the hell do I do now?" plunged into her brain and that feverish-nauseous trembling scattered over her entire body that hadn't subsided for over a week already—as though she really was a mechanical doll in which all the wheels and screws had slipped out of their grooves so that she could only swallow liquids and couldn't sleep at all for several nights at a time—it was only then that she turned to the mirror and saw it: coming up, coming up to the surface, artistically twisting her lips with their not yet totally smudged-off lipstick!—that same coldly ironic (it's a fuck party and nothing more) detached smile: what a story!—this smile said—God damn it, what a story...

And on that same night, as soon as she found herself alone (she felt better!), she finally, for the first time since his arrival, had a real dream: at first, still on the cusp of being awake and falling asleep, she had the one of him walking away from her on a narrow plank heading downward, but then there suddenly came a crowded, erotic nightmare: invisible hands, many hands caressing her from all sides—persistently, hotly, suffocatingly, and she had to gather all her strength to break free—only to turn up in a huge, empty, echoing hall with a high, vaulted ceilings like backstage at the opera, something akin to constructivist stage props were cluttering up the hall—carelessly draped pedestals, plinths of papier-mâché, some kind of stepladders, in a nave that looked like a dark cave stood a high podium, and flying in from all sides, with the whistle and rustle of wings and capes, settling on all those raised surfaces were the Princes and Princesses of Darkness—black vestments flitted by, out of the corner of her eye she spotted some chicken claws coming out of huge paws overgrown with shaggy reddish wool that had dug into a protruding section of a wall, but her main attention was glued to an incredibly tall—you couldn't even make out its face!—figure dressed in a black cassock standing at the podium: is that not the Grand Prince himself, she wondered, who decided to reveal himself? None of this was in the slightest bit frightening—despite all of the striking external trappings, the demonic assembly constituted no clear threat, rather it gave the impression of a ritual somewhat reminiscent of a Brezhnev-era party meeting and in fact treated her with a kind of friendly acceptance, taking her into its circle, accepting her as one of its own—and, walking up and down that filled hall from one end to the other she began, crossing herself confidently, to recite "Our Father," and they obediently transformed themselves into whorls of neon-blue vapor and flew off with a pyrotechnic hiss—only a gigantic cat, turning into a neon-blue shadow of a cat, hopped around from pedestal to pedestal for some time still before he too went up in smoke, and then there was still that panting gnome—with black wings, with a ski cap and simpleton's round face (clown nose!) who swooped in late and, not catching on to what's happening, lashed out at her, "What, hasn't it started yet?"—for him especially she repeated "Our Father" and he, after putting up some minimal resistance for appearances' sake, and likewise not presenting himself as *anything too scary* as he lunged for her a few times, had to, in the end, what else was there to do, also turn into a neon-blue ball and, releasing a carefree whistle, fly away. In that dream she first felt a waft of *relief*—as though she had returned back to herself and, all alone in the now emptied hall, she thought, no— she realized: so it's not really serious—this suicide stuff. At least, *it wasn't yet.*

Ladies and gentlemen, I feel a little awkward raising this issue now—obviously, it's more suited for a sermon than a serious academic paper, and I can see you, one after another, leaving the auditorium with sarcastically curled lips: "crazy stuff," typical Slavic mysticism, your auditorium seats noisily snapping back—just a moment, I'm asking for just one more minute of your attention, I've even prepared, just to keep things *comme il faut,* a quotation for you here—I apologize that it's not from Derrida, Foucault, or Lacan but quite the contrary, from Jacob Böhme: when Satan was asked why he left heaven, he replied that he wanted to be *an author.*

Ladies and gentlemen, in the country which from its inception was a human creation and where the authorship of each person over his or her own fate is the fundamental postulate of education (I have here a newspaper clipping: an elderly millionaire couple, the Browns—Richard, seventy-nine years old, and Helen, seventy-six—killed themselves by carbon dioxide poisoning in their garage, prior to that bequeathing their entire estate—ten million dollars, nothing to sneeze at!—to Christian charity and sending explanatory letters to their friends: both were gravely ill and after considering everything rationally they decided that rather than squandering the money they worked so hard for their whole lives on doctors and medical care it would be better to help young people get on their feet—will they also be buried outside the perimeter of the church cemetery, or will those who derive benefit from their millions intercede with their prayers to God and ultimately save their souls? It's a murky business—this dispensing with yourself as you see fit: there was a certain Father Kolbe in Auschwitz who during one of the "purges" there offered himself up to die in place of a certain Pole, because that man had two sons at home—the SS officer smirked and allowed the exchange, and that man survived and returned to his family in Warsaw only to find out that his two sons were killed during a bombardment, how about that!—ah, Father Kolbe, you interfered in something that wasn't your business, you wanted to become an author— and you broke the rules of the game, because that man was meant to die and who knows, if you hadn't meddled, his boys might still be alive today, and I am seriously concerned, that's right, don't laugh—I am concerned about the Browns' millions—will they really bring someone a luckier lot in life, or will, God forbid, one of those Brown fellowship recipients burn to a crisp in a chemical fire in the research lab where he ends up at their expense, or will yet another one, after completing his studies in Italy and becoming a renowned singer, after years of success and glory, slit his throat once he loses his voice? It's a shame, really, that your country has never known a proper war— war allows you to understand many things about life and death, because individual fates, no matter how telling, generally never teach you anything; a year ago, I remember, the latest news carried a hilarious, if you allow me to call it that, story: in New York some guy threw himself out of the window of a skyscraper, but landed on the roof of a parked automobile whole and unharmed, and, unwilling to accept defeat—obviously, he had been taught in childhood to get what he wanted no matter what—headed back up to that hundred and umpteenth floor and, if you can imagine, threw himself out again, this time breaking an arm, a leg, and something else, but still wasn't able, the poor sucker, to settle scores with his life—let's admit, ladies and gentlemen, that somewhere in the depths of our souls we are a bit annoyed by the arrogance of this bastard—just like we are by the burglar who tries to break down the door when he can't pick the lock, or by the spoiled child who stamps its foot and screams "gimme!"—so he didn't succeed, it's what he deserves)—in this country, ladies and gentlemen, with its increasing proliferation of satanic sects in the underground and psychiatric offices on the surface, might it not be time to stop and ponder over the question of *authorial rights*—over what we truly *can* do, and what we shouldn't?

Wanting to be an author—to create—is to raise your hand to the exclusive prerogative of God. Because none of us truly creates, ladies and gentlemen—we all remember the example about creative thinking from our psychology textbooks—a mermaid, half woman and half fish—what poverty of thought, if you really consider it, the imagination of a butcher—cut a piece from here and a piece from there, glue it together and we're all proud: we're artists! But what about *ex nihilo*—have you tried that? Can't do it? That's the point...All that we're given—like children toys—are ready-cut slivers of reality, fragments, details, colored pieces of some large, unsolvable puzzle, and we crawl over fussing with them, without raising our eyes, touching them, licking them, smelling them, a completely innocent and pleasant occupation—except that the point is that every once in a while (ho, you wouldn't believe how often, actually, and it doesn't necessarily take a genius) we manage to put a few of those puzzle pieces together according to some greater, taken from who-knows-where, invisible-to-the-naked-eye *plan*, in which one can recognize the pulsation of independent, as if naturally born, life. And that's when our authorial (ha-ha!) pride switches on: we puff out our chests, ruffle our feathers, and imagine ourselves to be creators—whereas all that has happened is that the curtain was pulled back for a second and through the slit we saw a tiny tip of the original *general plan*, the same one according to which *the world* was once created—from nothing, complete and beautiful, the one from which humanity backed away (when? at which prehistoric turn? in which Pyrenees cave?), and the memory of it (so evanescent! so distressingly easily lost! and yet—how would we live if we were to lose even that?), of that original, blinding completeness is preserved, besides religion, only in art and in love.

(I believe that all those rigorous clerics had a point—the iconoclasts, the Puritans, and the rest of them—that the very idea of an icon or a religious sculpture *profanes* the sacred—the joint venture of religion and art truly is a compromise on religion's part, an inevitable concession—from exhaustion—enough already!—because of an inability, any longer, to establish direct contact without resorting to various obvious vulgar devices: peeling gilding on wooden boards, an angel's nose chewed off by bad weather, a statuette crudely decorated with motley rags. Quite possibly at one time there had been direct contact—there had, but what's the point of trying to track it down now?... Religion, having become a social institution, has gone to the dogs— in church, where I dragged myself one day in the hope of somewhat dispersing the dark nimbus cloud that burned my brain day after day without allowing a single cooling thought to slip through, there reigned a distinct spirit of a closed society: curious glances at the stranger, clustering of old friends on the balcony after the service in separate groups, stares, laughter, meaningful exchanges, shared news—people showed up the way they would to a party, to "socialize," and praying in front of them felt somehow inappropriate.) *Right of access* to the plan is still maintained by us—individual access, because humanity itself over the past several hundred years has been moving further and further away, in leaps and bounds (perhaps beginning with the Renaissance, with Mirandola's audacious: "Man! Adam! I have put you in the center of the world!"—so go ahead and stand there, may you stand there till Kingdom Come, and now every psycho with a paralyzed arm thinks he's Adam while we afterward scratch our heads unable to tally the millions killed: was it twenty, or forty, or all the way up to sixty?)—while the memory of lost divine status keeps teasing us, it so-o entices us, flickering seductively, but too bad, as soon as we step a little closer, oops—yup, there he is, waiting at the door watching us and rubbing his paws—the One who would be Author—he'd so love to wedge his way in there and take over, but can't do it himself; only by riding in on our backs, on the backs of those *with access* can he get in there and that's why it's a hundred times safer for us not to even try anything, to forget all about access and play obediently in the sandbox, shuffling around those puzzle pieces, creating out of them newer and newer useless combinations—lining up Campbell's soup cans in a row, displaying rubber chairs dressed in women's shoes at the Biennale, blowing streams of soap bubbles onto newspaper pages—identical, meaningless words, sometimes it ends up being quite entertaining, kilometers of texts (that's right, not poems anymore, *texts*) about your first ride on a bicycle, about your first period, or about nothing at all—it's okay, "interesting," cackles the gaggle of critics, university professors, doctors of literature, forgive me if I've offended anyone present—they say that if you seat three monkeys at a typewriter that between now and eternity they have a chance of clicking out a *Hamlet* for us, ladies and gentlemen, I'm going to reveal a terrible secret to you now: art in our times is slowly going to the dogs because—it's *afraid.*

Only love protects us from fear: only it alone can shield us, and if we carry it within us, then...then...(I honestly don't know *what* then, I don't know what will happen now with that man, what more destruction will be wrought by that black tornado with a slight, phosphorus-pale figure locked in an iron grip getting pummeled in its vortex—a "devil's wedding" on dusty fall roads, my grandmother used to tell me: if you see it, step aside, she herself still knew how to throw a knife horizontally through the eye of the whirlwind, and then blood would show on the knife, all that we know how to do these days is perhaps whip a knife across the kitchen at the man we love—the gesture seems to be the same—a copy, an imitation, a reflex of tribal memory with its inner meaning dead, a gesture with which, rather than shield yourself, you throw yourself into the very center of the "devil's wedding." You mustn't, oh you mustn't chase the cold starlight of *loveless* beauty: those aren't the allies you want on this path.

Blinding, wonderful, and wild!
Glitter your lights, seduce and entice
Toward speed, invisible rivers
Only—Lord!—don't deceive me:
Don't slip out from underfoot like dry weed
At the moment of frightening union
With your radiance—don't become emptiness:
Musty scent of brittle garbage
(Like a trap disguised by the devil
to appear like a treasure...) And
in hell, at the bottom,
The nothingness of my vacuous days,
Wasted by gnawing ache, will burn yellow!
Every punishment I will take as a blessing
Only, Heavenly Powers, not this:
From Ukrainian Hades, spare me,
From the forcible dying alive
Without hope, without deeds, without time,

In emptiness, lost in space—out there
Where still rot, after the hundreds of misfortunates,
Remains of that which was meant to—spring to life
Jumping forward, out of its skin
Tearing skin off hands and feet as it goes
Like a condemned soul from under
   the executioner's axe
Toward eternal careening flames

—that's the sort of stuff I was writing, I finally got my wish, so to speak, look at me—Lady Dante! Yet Dante not only had Virgil, he also had Beatrice. And if there is no love living inside us at all times then, instead of expanding, the tunnel through which we race with such excitement grows narrower and narrower, it becomes harder and harder to squeeze through, and we no longer fly, as it seemed at first, but crawl with great effort, coughing up clumps of our own lungs and also that, which was once called our gift and which, my God, really *was* a gift!—and we ooze onto canvases like squashed bugs, with the colorful spots of our own poison, and we choke on carrion words that stink of rot and hospital carbolic acid, and all kinds of unpleasant things begin to happen to us, insane asylums and prisons show up on the horizon (depending on your luck), and then the only thing remaining is to jump off a bridge (Paul Celan), tie a noose around your neck in the hallway of someone's house (Marina Tsvetaeva), stick your head into a gas oven (Sylvia Plath), lock yourself in a garage, maximizing emissions from an exhaust pipe (Ann Sexton), swim out to sea as far as possible (Ingrid Jonker), the count goes on, "to be continued," so what do you think, is this normal, is this the way things should be? But the further you go on, the worse it is for these "things," nobody *lives to see their "Faust"* anymore, what do you think, this is a coincidence, you think that people have less talent these days?...It's their chances that are decreasing, chances are decreasing for all of us.

Only love protects us from fear. But who (what) will protect love itself from fear?

(And there are more and more sex shops with every year, mechanical devices, oh, these advantages of the technological age, sex over the telephone, they got me that way once, too—at home, in my own home, where did you think: took me for a ride totally, never did find out who it was—at first a female voice disguised as a whisper—I took it to be a friend, a pretty screwed-up gal: "Olka? Is that you?"—it was no Olka, as it turned out later, even though that thing seemed to confirm: yeah, me—and they began the scam: I'm in trouble, I'm calling from someone's apartment: there's two guys here, they say they want to rape me—either in the bum or in the mouth, there's one of them coming now, I'm scared, "Where are you? I'll call the police, give me your address!" but the non-Olka was gone and instead a young male voice, breathing threateningly, came on the line: "You're her friend, right? You want me to let her go? Then moan for me"—what wouldn't you do for a dear friend in trouble, it was disgusting—I tried to plug in my sense of humor, it's okay, it's like they're asking you to sing a little song for them, but when finally, in reply to my helplessly painful cry of humiliation [you're screaming from the abuse and they think it's from pleasure, or maybe they're not thinking that at all, maybe your pain is exactly what it takes to make them come?] the male voice abruptly snapped, "Done," and a busy signal came in on the receiver, short beeps like drops of water from a leaky tap, I, wiping my moist forehead, nonetheless felt—laughs aside—raped: that was a young healthy man on the line, could it be that, damn it, he, too, was *afraid* of a live woman?)

Fear came early. Fear was passed on in the genes, one was to fear all beyond the immediate family circle—anyone who expressed any degree of interest in you was in fact spying for the KGB to find out what's really going on at home and then those bad men will come again and put Daddy in prison. Especially suspect were those who tried to strike up "liberal" conversations. Around ninth grade, at the citywide Creative Writing Olympiad she met a whiz kid in big glasses from the math school. He had the skin of a freshly-peeled peach, rare for an adolescent, and glancing at him sideways she could see, behind the abnormally thick lenses, dark feminine eyelashes as thick as silk; and when he laughed, his whole body contracted as often happens with very nervous intellectual boys who aren't allowed to go out to play by themselves, but are let out only when sitting on a sled bundled up in a wool shawl to well above the bridge of the nose. Such boys inevitably fell in love with her, that much couldn't be helped, but in spite of it they were avid readers and liked to discuss what they read. And so one day the whiz kid from the math school, holding on to her elbow awkwardly and old-fashionedly (as if with an artificial limb) while he guided her around the slippery spots—it was winter then and the snow-covered sidewalks glistened with treacherous black mirrors—had the indiscretion to ask, by the way, had she read the banned Ukrainian author Vynnychenko? Instantly she felt her head pound: This is it! This is what Mother and Father warned about—and with that shrewd Lenin glint in her eye (she did sense it quite consciously to be Lenin's), accompanied by oh, such a languorous pause as if to say, okay, let's play with this, I can see right through you, she replied, "No, can't say that I have," and, having waited it out until the whiz kid confessed all he knew—about the democratic Ukrainian republic that waged war on the Soviets, about the Ukrainians living abroad (as she listened, practically swooning at such flirtation with danger, she no longer had the slightest doubt *who* this was talking to her)—she doused him with a bucket of ice, tapping out each syllable in precise Pioneer Girl fashion ("Attention!" "Right face!" "Forward... march!") informing him that she hadn't the slightest interest in émigré counterrevolutionary trash, and at a time when the international situation is as tense and complicated as it is and demands our vigilance, she has always been outraged by young people who listen to Voice-of-this and Voice-of-that radio broadcasts—he, staring wildly at her with both pairs of eyes seemed to forget all about breathing ("Little hedgehog, where was your head? Forgot to breathe, and now you're dead!")—that'll teach him! She was more pleased with herself than ever before: her first test of maturity and she passed it without a hitch! No, she had always said she would never want to relive her adolescence—those desperate, unconscious attempts to *break out*—out of the dull concrete walls, out of the family nest choked inside, amid billows of pungent fear, miasmic haze, where one false move, one ill-considered revelation, and you splash into the murky waters to your death. On the radio that Father listened to every evening, squeezing ear-first into the speaker that sputtered with a deafening scrape and occasionally burst into a sharp, dangerously increasing metallic whistle—on the radio came memoirs of the dying Snegirov, lists of surgically removed intestines, ruptured kidneys and bladders, insulin shocks, forcibly inserted feeding tubes, puddles of blood and vomit on cement floors—summary reports from the slaughterhouse, a carving of carcasses: Marchenko, Stus, Popadiuk, every few weeks more names, young and handsome, youths not much older than yourself with thick manes of hair brushed back stiffly, you dreamed of them the way your girlfriends dreamed of movie stars, any day now he'll come out of prison bearing scars and a mature masculinity, and you'll meet—except that they never came out and the airwaves groaned with their agony, while Father sat on the other side listening helplessly, year after year, ever since the day he himself was thrown out of work, just sat in the house and listened to the radio. There *was* no breaking out—all around nothing but Communist Youth League meetings, political education classes, and the Russian language. One only ventured out there (like a four-year-old to a stool in the middle of the room to recite a poem for aunties and uncles) in order to reproduce, in ringing tones and tape-recorder accuracy, all that had been learned from them and them alone, and only this guaranteed *safety*—a Gold Medal on leaving high school, a Diploma of Red Distinction

at university, and then ever so carefully along the tightrope—my God, all the garbage she had let pass through
her brain!—and at age fifteen tumbling right into a depression, complaining of mysterious stomach pains, Daddy ran
himself off his feet dragging her from doctor to doctor
who found nothing wrong, for days she tossed in bed crying hysterically from the slightest sharp word—Daddy's
girl, apple of his eye, it was he who hovered, wings outstretched, over her first menstruation, calmly explaining
that this is very good, this is what happens to all girls, just
lie and rest, don't get up. He brought her thinly sliced
apples laid out on a saucer, like for a real sick girl, and so
she lay there, curled up and very still, frightened by this
new feeling—on the one hand shame at her secret being
revealed so openly (but then how can you have secrets from
Daddy?) and, on the other, a kind of searing vulnerability,
a wary uncertainty—a feeling that would reappear at the
loss of virginity (which she only manages after Daddy's
death), and then every time after that, the same eternal
sense of daughterly duty, ultimate feminine *submission* from
which men, not having a clue of its source, would necessarily go wild (*"You're such a good fuck!"*) and then she would
leave them. Break loose, that's all she wanted to do, break
loose—all elbows from spontaneous adolescent growth,
pimply teenager in tears at her own awkwardness, one pair
of panty hose speckled with brown knots where she tried
to sew up the runs, and one dress, the school uniform worn
lily-white at the elbows. She went to school dances reli-
giously—every Friday without fail, like a Moslem to the
mosque!—in a borrowed blouse and too-short skirt from
her Pioneer Girl days (white top, black bottom), consuming

herself with bitter envy at the sight of her classmates in all-grown-up clothes, with grown-up haircuts done at the stylist's, in full bloom like the proverbial cherry orchard, glistening in high-gloss lipstick and black Lancôme butterfly lashes—ten roubles was what that blue tube of mascara cost, and Mother's monthly paycheck, on which the three of them lived, came out to 150 roubles, so what was there to do but *steal* it, in the coatroom, from a briefcase thoughtlessly left open by a beauty queen from the senior class—true, it was a pretty cheap tube, from Poland, half used up, or so she consoled herself, and not such a great loss for the beauty queen, but nonetheless there it was, nineteenth century, the classic Jean Valjean loaf of bread and Cosette staring at the doll-store window: shame, fear, a secret, both despicable and exciting, like her exhibitionist exercises alone in front of the mirror. She applied makeup badly in the school bathroom, painting crooked lines under her eyes, and after the dance she would fiercely scrub the mascara from her red eyelids: it was frightening to think what would happen if Daddy saw—Daddy, who was always so afraid for her, who ran around collecting dossiers on each of her girlfriends: they were all spoiled, smoked, and kissed boys, Daddy screamed, face turning beet-red and she, you have to hand it to her, screamed just as loud in return, and then sobbed in the bathroom—especially after that memorable evening when he slapped her face right out on the street, at the trolley stop, because she had taken off somewhere and he decided that she was running away from him—but she came back, because there *was* nowhere to run to, and he, not saying a word, slapped her as hard as he could across the face. Of course, later there were hugs-and-kisses, forgiveness-begging and the like, "my baby," "my golden girl," all this after several red-hot hours of pandemonium, wailing, sobbing, slamming of doors, accompanied by the shuffle of Mother's feeble attempts to intervene—because Mother was quite beside the point in all this, Mother was, in fact, frigid, and obviously out of it, a black windowpane deflecting all light (later on, one morning in the early months of your marriage, she would poke her head into your bedroom with an alarm clock ringing merrily in her hands: wakey, wakey, breakfast is ready!—precisely at *the* moment—and after the ensuing explosive scene she would weep like an orphan in the kitchen, frightened and helpless: she was just trying her best!—so that in the end you, having calmed yourself and shaken the rest of the shivers from your startled body, would be apologizing and cheering her up). And what else could she have been if not frigid, a child-survivor of the Famine (a three-year-old in 1933, she stopped walking, while Grandmother made her way to Moscow in freight cars, switching from train to train, in order to exchange her dowry—two thick strands of Mediterranean pearls—for two bags of dry bread). A child nourished on single stalks of wheat stolen from the field, for which the collective farm guard, catching her once, cut her across the face with a whip—you can still see a thin white thread of a scar even now—and it was lucky to have ended with that, because her father, your grandfather, that is, was already up in the Arctic panning gold in a slave-gang, and about fifteen years later *your* father, her future husband, would be up there doing the same. And as for her, she made out okay, she got over the stolen ears of wheat and finally got enough to eat, twenty years or so later once she graduated from university and found a job—and American Sovietologists still can't figure out why there are so many fat, shapeless women in this generation, they read Fromm and Jung up and down and between the lines—*Eat,* that's what these babes wanted to do when they hit twenty—*eat, that's all!*—stuff their faces with meager bread rations in student dorms, both hands, picking up crumbs, what a clitoris was they never did get to find out (it hit you for the first time standing in line at a pharmacy: they had brought in some menstrual pads, and a queue made up entirely of young women was busily stuffing shopping bags—the grannies, meantime, walked up shyly: "Girls, what's in those packages?"—"They're women's packages, for women!" the girls snarled back: not for the likes of you, in other words—and the grannies stared back blankly, not understanding). So Mother was as innocent as a lamb, or rather the Virgin Mary (there really was something Madonna-like about her in those photos from the late fifties—the time when they all finally did get enough to eat—she glowed with such gentle innocence, a girl in curls, you couldn't take your eyes off her!— delicate long face with a slim tapered nose—a now lost, quiet kind of beauty illuminated by an inner smile, the Cossack Baroque portrait three hundred years later: Roxolana, Varvara Apostol, Varvara Langyshivna—yup, those were the days, now gone for sure! You still get to see the full-faced, embroidered, fresh-off-the-farm-let's-go- dance-in-the-cherry-orchard variety, but not the true Cossack ladies, forget about those! And even your own good looks are already by two exponents coarser, more vulgar—let's not forget to make that *were*). And so Mother,

gentle songbird, sacrificial lamb, slaved over her dissertation in a Khrushchev communal housing project, while in
the kitchen her neighbor, a cook from the local working-
class diner—one of those that Lenin had ordained to rule
the state—(single mother of five from five different men),
threw rags and teeth into Mother's borsch (baby teeth
belonging to one of the progeny, perhaps?). But Mother
did finish her dissertation in poetics despite it all, right in
time for 1973, when as the spouse of an "unreliable" she
was booted the hell out of grad school, so that the day of
your dissertation defense (which you needed like a hole in
the head) was in fact *her* day, she was as happy as a child:
"Ah, if only your father were alive to see this!"—and *how*
in God's name, by what means was he supposed to have
stayed alive, pitched to the very bottom of the well but
catching hold of a beam on the way down in a spasmodic
grip and clinging desperately (anything but back to the
prison camp), buried alive in four walls, listening to the
radio, blowing cigarette smoke out of the tiny pilot window
and watching with horror as the only woman of his life,
his own flesh and blood, irrevocably slipped away, pushing
out through the trap door, propelled by the sheer force of
natural growth: *"Lift up your nightie, I want to see how you've
been growing"* (and would it not be the same kind of both
concerned and authoritative intonation twenty years later—
"Turn around, I want to take you from behind now"—that would
awaken in you that long-forgotten feeling of home?)—and
it won't matter that you never liked it from behind, it won't
matter that at first you refused to lift up your nightie,
flushed with an un-childlike feeling of insult—only to hear
in response a quiet and unfamiliarly moist, deeply-felt "my

child, it's me, your Daddy!"—in the end result of which the
nightie did indeed go up (what else could you do?)—that
anxious, obscene feeling of exposure, the first experience,
far stronger than any of that knee-touching under the
classroom desk—and yet you yearned to break free, God
how you yearned to break free—like a condemned soul
from under the executioner's axe, but—where? To your
teenage friends, any dance in sight, rock bands, football
games, and the first groping of body parts in the darkness
of the school gym—what a joke! You couldn't even tell any
of them how in the third year *they* finally showed up, your
father's fear came to pass, because fear—it always reifies
in the end. They burst inside the four family walls like a
tornado with a luscious creak of leather holster belts and
a vigorous outdoor wind behind them and suddenly filled
the room to capacity: three huge males, rosy-cheeked from
the sub-zero temperatures, slapping the covers of their
identity cards, "pack up, let's get going!" Father scurried
around looking for papers, sorting something on his desk,
hands trembling, stunned and pathetic, and then *you*
jumped out at them from the corner of the room, pimply
pale-green adolescence trying to unbend its back—
squelched and squeaky, long bangs swinging across your
nose, you screeched: "How dare you, what right do you
have!" It didn't come off too well, actually it came off not
well at all, the guys shut you up as easily as kicking a puppy
aside with one foot (young junior officer, moustache the
hint of a thin line was trying real hard, piece of fucking
shit on his first responsible assignment—no piddly matter,
catching a real-live anti-Soviet!—"not your business,
sweetie, you're a little young for this, aren't you?"). And

anyway, your parents, dark-faced with terror as though someone had slipped Polaroid paper under their skin, began hissing-shushing-flapping long before you even rushed forward. But the first failure didn't stop you, because it's true what the man said, you're a brave woman, that you are, sweetness. Some years later, as a student in the eighties out on a date with the latest cutie-pie, you decided to head for the theater with a group of friends to see some hit show in from Moscow. Just a random attempt since nobody had tickets, laughing your heads off the whole while, quips flying back and forth like snowballs, you began storming the ticket office with a mob of similar revelers, the crowd having grown quite sizable by then: New Year's Eve after all, you're young and alive and who wants to go home and that's when the cops showed up—a squadron of paddy wagons revved up, gray coats plowed into the throng sending furrows of breaker waves crashing in all directions and who the hell even knows how it happened, just a moment ago there you were, well, having fun—so, if you hadn't gotten in, big deal, you would have headed over to Khreshchatyk for a cup of Turkish coffee! When suddenly there was cutie-pie's friend, the most persistent of the bunch, light and slippery as quicksilver—in fact, one more push and he just might have squeezed into the theater!—there he was, identified and fished out from the huddled, bellowing herd and now being dragged under the arms by two gorillas in uniform. He couldn't even reach the asphalt with his feet, the rest of your coterie followed in confusion, not having the foggiest of where to begin, and he was already whining to the gorillas: "Come on, guys, let go of me, let me go, please, come on, guys," legs twisting in the air independently of his torso, and your cutie-pie, dumb jerk, shuffled behind like a somnambulist mumbling—"It's okay, they won't do nothing to him"—meantime the paddy wagon was standing ready, rear end wide open and then you once again—brave woman!—with a panther leap of a by now considerably stronger and better-looking body landed smack in front of the wagon, a long-legged lightning streak in a short sheepskin jacket, scattering them to both sides (by that time they were already pushing the poor schmuck into the van): "Boys!"—your voice sent sparks through the air like a piece of flint— "What are you trying to do here, huh?!" And you sprang the captive free: the *boys* (more like mating bulls, really) opened ranks, became somehow softer around the edges and more malleable, stepped back, mumbled something in defense along the lines of "Well, how come he…"—oh yeah, he resisted arrest and said something rude—and then cutie-pie stepped forward and you scooped up the victim and let's get the hell out of here! (And wouldn't it be like that on your first night with that man, when he boldly zoomed up the one-way street and the cops pulled him over—and he, puny and stooped in an unbuttoned leather jacket which suddenly drooped on him like a used condom, was explaining something to them out there, flailing his arms about: come on, guys, what did I do, I didn't, honest—and you, tired of waiting in the car swung the door open, stepped out, click-clicked your heels down the sidewalk, tossed your curls and, absorbing the ravenous glances of the holster-swinging males—one could light a cigarette on your scintillating laugh: "What's the problem, gentlemen? We didn't break any rules?"—and the tempest somehow dissipated all at once, well okay then, go ahead, but watch yourselves. And in the early morning, fixing his shining eyes on you as you lay half-draped on the couch, he muttered slowly, smacking his lips and relishing his triumphant smile: *"Ah, you're a tough broad—jumped right out to plow the cops in the kisser...I could go do some jobs with you,"* and you were flooded by a surge of childish pride: Finally, finally somebody noticed—because he *was* one of those who could have come out of the prison camps and you met, after all these years—for he was more than a brother, he was homeland and home...) Fear oozed in from the outside like caustic fumes, but inside the house it was warm, sultry in fact, teenage depression, no, neurasthenia, some kind of stupid pills, fever stuck at 99.2, tears umpteen times a day, the lady doctor told you to undress and asked Daddy to leave the room "she's a big girl already"—and you were shocked that Daddy, rather than defend his paternal rights—after all, it was *his* child that was about to be examined!—shuffled to the door in humiliation, flustered and dwarfed as if caught red-handed (the curious thing, she tells herself with the imperturbability of a surgeon, is that he really was a good-looking guy, talkative, witty, and ready to embrace life, and women liked him, and there would have been absolutely no problem finding some action outside the house, so why did he guard his chastity like some Galician old maid, was it not because Mother married him still *before* he was "rehabilitated" and he spent his whole life cowering, afraid to hear her say aloud what he was secretly tormenting himself with within—that he ruined her life? But to be left alone, *without* her, he was afraid of that, too, wasn't he). And by way, this time they only charged him with "willful unemployment," keeping him for only twenty-four hours in the district jail and sending him out after that only as a night watchman to a construction site where he sat in a glass booth opening gates for dump trucks and the rest of the time reading Bruno Schulz, about whom he was going to someday write a book but never did get around to it (he had pretty good taste in literature, except that he couldn't stand any hint of eroticism, like the Catholic Index)—his panic at her unrestrained growth—"Hey, stop that!"—settled into his insides and slowly sawed away at them with a dull blade, but they only diagnosed cancer when it was too late to operate, his whole reproductive system was affected: prostate, testes (every day Mother grated carrots for juice and squeezed them by hand, twisting the ball of mash through a piece of cheesecloth, her fingers, which had once strummed a guitar, acquired a permanent yellow color and could be straightened only with effort, and at nights Daddy's girl would run to the phone booth down the block to call the ambulance, and so when Mother, her eyes white with horror, returned from the hospital one day with news of the diagnosis, which at all costs was to be kept a secret from Daddy, the first thought that flashed through your head [which you would never ever forgive yourself], was a cold and merciless, hissed through clenched teeth: Thank God!). In fact, it was nothing less than war, a war in which there could be no winners because, having exhausted all means to get his way (pin 'em down with your knee, shove 'em into the crib, "she's just a child," we wanted a boy, but that's okay, she turned out a smart tough cookie and she'll *show them all!*)—having done all that, the man resorts to the ultimate weapon, death, and that does the trick, you lay down your arms and you go over to his side. And your adolescence, which you swore you would never again relive, it catches up with you twenty years later, releasing from the darkest recesses of your being a tearful and frightened teenage girl who takes over completely, and then it laughs at you long and hard: "What, thought you could get away?... Didn't get too far, did you?"

Maybe it's true that *slaves should not bear children*, she muses, staring dully out the window: yesterday the first snow fell, but now it's melted, only the windshields of cars parked up and down the street look like wet spots on newborn calves. A man—black skin, bright red jacket, blue baseball cap—bounces down the sidewalk with his hands in his pockets: it must have gotten colder. Because what is slavery, if not infection by fear—she draws toward her an open notebook half-filled with such lukewarm aphorisms that move you about as much as a textbook in formal logic. Slavery is the state of being infected by fear. And fear kills love. And without love—children, poems, paintings—all is pregnant with death. A+, girl! You have completed your research.

Ladies and gentlemen—no, for now it's just ladies or, more precisely, one lady, Donna from East European Studies, one of the few friends you've made during this time, half-Irish, half-Slavic mix, a rather pleasing combination: golden hair, warm hazel eyes, high cheekbones, skin sprinkled with fine freckles like a good sesame seed roll. You can't smoke in the university cafeteria where you arranged to meet for lunch, and Donna, having finished her cup of the dark brown liquid Americans for some reason insist on calling coffee, stuffs a stick of chewing gum in her mouth: sublimated nicotine. This chewing of the cud comes off as not at all offensive, perhaps because Donna laughs so often and so sincerely, which gives the impression that she keeps tasting something funny. She's writing a dissertation on gender in postcommunist politics, she is quite honestly interested in knowing why in those politics there aren't and never have been any women—a question that stumps you every time, no matter how often it's posed to you by Western intellectuals (hell, how am I supposed to know?). It seems that Donna suspects that this is the root of all our problems: like all feminists, she is convinced that men are "full of shit," and the minute you let them loose you've got wars all over the place, concentration camps, famine, natural disasters, someone starts shutting off the hot water and electricity, then there are budget cuts in the department for the second year in a row and her dissertation defense is postponed yet again. And so Donna takes your story perhaps not so much to heart, as directly into her files. Ladies and gentlemen, let me go on.

"Whaat?!" Donna thrusts herself forward so that her golden curls bounce in the air and settle into the deep cut of her sweater.

"How?!" Donna is outraged. "How could he do that? And how can anybody treat a woman that way?!"

"Oh my!" Donna nods her head sympathetically and with completely uncharacteristic domesticity begins straightening out a nonexistent tablecloth with the palms of both hands: a gesture that indicates complete bewilderment and a loss for appropriate commentary. No, she had problems with her last boyfriend, but nothing like this!...

"Listen," says Donna as her face clears up with the discovery of a solution: "Looks like this guy is severely sick, don't you think?"

A short course in psychology, the road to mental health: find the reason and the problem goes away. Why hasn't anyone thought of doing this with nations: you neatly psychoanalyze a whole national history, and "poof, you're cured." Literature as a form of national therapy. Hmm, not a bad idea. Too bad that we happen to have no literature.

"I just don't understand one thing," Donna says judgmentally (it's obvious that a fundamental aspect of her worldview is at stake here). "I don't understand, why did you put up with it? In bed, I mean? Why didn't you just say no?"

The conceptual approach: women's struggle for their rights.

What can I tell you, Donna-dearest. That we were raised by men fucked from all ends every which way? That later we ourselves screwed the same kind of guys, and that in both cases they were doing to us what others, *the others*, had done to them? And that we accepted them and loved them as they were, because not to accept them was to go over to the others, the other side? And that our only choice, therefore, was and still remains between victim and executioner: between nonexistence and an existence that kills you.

After throwing the vestiges of their lunch into the cafeteria trash bin—plastic trays with paper dishware:

cups and plates all in bright spots from different sauces—
soy, ketchup, mustard, plum (vermilion, carmine, ochre,
umber)—palettes, props from a theatrical performance
(act one: an artist's studio; act two: a room in a student
dorm; act three cancelled for technical reasons, tickets
not returned and prayers not answered)—they head for
the exit. Donna pushes the glass doors, a sudden burst of
frosty air joyfully zaps the lungs, cars drive by, young men
in jackets sporting emblems of their university walk past
laughing, a disturbing electric-blue sky blazes overhead,
and on the corner a tall, shaggy, gray-haired Leonardo
da Vinci stands wrapped in a blanket, stretching a paper
Coca-Cola cup toward them and rattling coins: "Help the
homeless, ma'am!"—"I'm homeless myself," she shakes her
head, not at him, out into space.

"But you know," Donna turns to her suddenly as she pulls
on her fine leather driving gloves and happily chews on a
new stick of gum, "these East European men of yours may be
brutal at times, but at least they're passionate. While ours..."

...And you'll be staring out of the airplane window watching the suitcases go up the conveyer belt of the ramp
loader and disappear into the bowels of the plane, one
after another, and then it will be just empty space float-
ing by, and the man with US Air written on his cap will
hop into the blackness of the baggage cart tug, and the
bag carts will move out, and while you follow them with
your eyes the ramp loader will be taken away and only a
gray puddle of melted snow will remain on the cement:
"Well, that's it," will resound in your head, like a cry in an

abandoned church, that's it—it means they have battened down the hatches, and in a moment you will hear the dry crackle of a microphone, "Ladies and gentlemen," the flight attendant will purr, and the plane will rumble and shake as the engines warm up, and soon you will be in a different reality, a different life, with the bitterly searing pain of unfulfillment of the life lived thus far ("qu'as tu fait, qu'as tu fait de ta vie?" a faraway voice will ask—ah, let's drop it, this topic's as old as life itself: you're always waiting, dreaming, thrashing about, hoping for something up ahead, and then one day you discover that this indeed *was* your life)—better for that pain to shut its mouth and not poke its nose out again.

Pass me the microphone and I'll say, "Ladies and gentlemen, we have created a wonderful world, and please accept, on this occasion, sincere greetings from US Air, and from CNN, and from the CIA, and the Uruguay drug mafia, and the Romanian Securitate, and from the Central Committee of the Communist Party of China, and from the millions of killers in all the prisons of the world as well as the tens of millions still at large, and from the five thousand Sarajevo children born of rape, who will, after all, grow up some day, and—onward and upward, brave new world, and that, actually, is all I wanted to say, thank you for your attention, ladies and gentlemen, have a good flight."

When I was young, I dreamed of such a death: plane crash over the Atlantic, an aircraft dissolving in the air and the ocean—no grave, no trace. Now I wish with all my heart that the plane land safely: I like to watch the tall, sinewy old man with the hooked nose and deeply furrowed lines running down from his eyes, the way he takes the nylon bag with a tennis racket on its gut and pushes it into the overhead bin; and the Spanish-looking brunette with the unbuttoned leather coat—she's on board with two children and while she removes the smaller one from her backpack carrier and sets him on the chair, the other one, a girl of about five, narrow tanned face in a baroque frame of promisingly capricious curls, flashes her eyes and her smile up and down the aisle in all directions, glowing with excitement—her first trip!—and her eyes stop on me:

"Hi!" she shouts happily.

"Hello there!" say I.

Pittsburgh, September–December, 1994

ABOUT THE AUTHOR

 Oksana Zabuzhko was born in 1960 in Ukraine. She made her poetry debut at the age of twelve, yet, because her parents had been blacklisted during the Soviet purges of the 1970s, it was not until the perestroika that her first book was published. She graduated from the department of philosophy of Kyiv Shevchenko University, obtained her PhD in philosophy of arts, and has spent some time in the USA lecturing as a Fulbright Fellow and a Writer-in-Residence at Penn State University, Harvard University, and University of Pittsburgh. After the publication of her novel *Fieldwork in Ukrainian Sex* (1996), which in 2006 was named "the most influential Ukrainian book for the fifteen years of independence," she has been living in Kyiv as a freelance author. She has authored seventeen books of poetry, fiction, and nonfiction, which have been translated into fifteen languages. Among her numerous acknowledgments are the Global Commitment Foundation Poetry Prize (1997), the MacArthur Grant (2002), the Antonovych International Foundation Prize (2008), the Ukrainian National Award, the Order of Princess Olha (2009), and many other national awards.

ABOUT THE TRANSLATOR

Halyna Hryn is an author, translator, editor, and researcher. She is the editor of *Hunger by Design: The Great Ukrainian Famine and Its Soviet Context*, translator of the novels *Peltse* and *Pentameron* by Volodymyr Dibrova, editor of the journal *Harvard Ukrainian Studies*, and a lecturer at Harvard's Department of Slavic Languages and Literatures. She received her PhD from the University of Toronto. Her research interests center on Soviet Ukrainian literature and cultural politics of the 1920s.